Oscar Brady

for Momo

1

Sam

When I come to, I'm in a room I don't recognize. My limbs are all bound to the posts of a dingy bed, my body spread out like a star. I ache all over, especially my head. I'm naked and I feel soiled. I have trouble remembering what happened or how I got here. In another room, I can hear a baby wailing and it takes me a brief moment to recognize my own child. Instinctually, I try to jerk out of bed, intending to follow the sound of my baby— *Emma!* —scooping her up and consoling her, as I've done on so many nights before, but I only make the ropes binding my wrists and ankles tighter.

I hear someone walking in another room, to my baby, to Emma. Whoever it is sounds like a woman when she talks, baby talk it sounds like. I try to twist my wrists out of the loops of knotted and frayed rope but this does nothing. "Hello?" I call out and the talking stops, but Emma continues crying.

Footsteps approach and I turn my head toward the only door to the room. I can't help but count—*one, two, three, four*—locks being undone before the door opens. A young woman that I've never seen before is carrying Emma. Emma's face is deep red. Who knows how long she's been crying. I can tell by the tone and inflection of her wails that she's hungry.

"She's hungry," the woman says as she walks to the bed. She's at most twenty years old, petite, and has a bedhead mane of dirty-blonde hair. She's only wearing a Poison band t-shirt and a pair of panties, which appear to be just as dingy as the bed. She holds a lit cigarette loosely in her lips as she marches to the bed and plops Emma onto my chest. I'm taken back to when Emma was born, how the nurse had slapped the wet, screaming newborn infant onto my chest for bonding. My childbirth pain was momentarily forgotten as I felt the immense and sudden love overwhelm me. The stranger moves Emma's head to get her to latch onto my right breast, and then sits in a chair in the corner of the room. The feet of the chair scrape against the floor as she sits. She taps the ash of her cigarette into a coffee cup on a small table near the chair and stares at me with half-lidded eyes as if measuring me.

I'm not sure if she's trying to intimidate me, but having my Emma-Bear on me immediately settles my nerves. I breathe out. "Who are you?" I ask, choking a bit on the words as I try to sound as calm as possible.

The blonde takes another drag and blows a large cloud of smoke toward me and Emma. "Not important." She smiles with teeth that are stained yellow and taps her cigarette into the mug again.

Normally, I would cradle Emma when I feed her, but with my arms tied, I can only twist slightly left and right to keep her balanced on the center of my torso. She's three months old and can only lift her head for a second or two and wriggle her body, which isn't too far off from my limited movement. "Can you at least tell me why I'm here? Or where I am?"

The young woman grins again and takes another drag of her waning cigarette, which she uses to light another that was tucked in her shirt sleeve. She looks like she was about to give me an answer but instead just says, "And why spoil the fun?"

"I can get you money. My husband makes a lot of money. Wall Street." A partial lie. Jared and I do well enough, but we aren't rich by any means. Thinking of Jared starts to bring back memories of what I was doing shortly before ending up on this bed, something about a deer. I was driving with Emma in the car. I remember Emma babbling, as if conversing with the passing trees in her window. I had to go a long way, and Jared wasn't there, just me and my Emma-Bear. I remember he had a reason for not coming, or at least he claimed to have a reason.

The cigarettes that the woman is smoking brings back a need. I kicked the habit when I found out I was pregnant. At first, the cravings were a challenge, but I never gave in, because I had a very good reason to quit. Now I need one.

The blonde clocks me looking at the cigarette. "Want one?" She says, still smirking. She has a thick country accent. "You know, it's really bad for the baby." She chuckles to herself and blows smoke in my direction again. "She's so cute, ain't she?" Her grin is devilish. "I could just eat her up!"

As if on cue, Emma drops my nipple and her mouth lolls. Normally when this happens, I would cradle her head back onto my breast and encourage her to continue feeding. I like to overfeed Emma because then she'll be conked out and I can take a nap or get some chores done. With my hands bound I can only look down at Emma, helpless. I can't even crane my neck to kiss Emma on the top of her head. Emma mouths, seeking my breast, but she can't lift her head well so she just lays there, looking like a fish gasping for air.

"Alright, she's done," the blonde says. She snubs out her cigarette then scoops Emma from me and struts toward the door.

"Wait!" I'm crying. The woman halts but doesn't turn around. A stifled "Please" is all I can muster.

"Don't worry, you'll see her again when she's hungry." The woman rocks Emma and shushes her though my baby isn't making any sounds, a bit milk-drunk. She turns back to me and shouts "Mooooo!" before breaking into laughter. The loud noise causes Emma to spasm but she quickly falls back to sleep. The woman shuts and locks the door behind her—*click, click, click, click*—leaving me to be alone once more.

I survey the room, trying to get an understanding of my environment. There's a window, but it's covered with a plywood board, which has gaps and holes, letting some light peek through. There is only the one door which leads out, no closet nor bathroom. There's the bed that I'm tied to, the chair which the blonde sat in, and two small tables, one by the chair and one by the bed. The one by the chair has an off-white coffee mug which the woman was using as an ashtray, and a small book which looks like a pulp romance. The table next to the bed has a cup of what I can only guess—hope—to be water and a bowl with what looks to be moldy stew.

I was right to suspect that I've soiled myself. Now that my senses are returning, I can tell that I must have peed in the bed while I was out, and now I'm just lying in my own filth, which makes things so much worse. I hate being dirty. I've hated being dirty since I was a kid. Jared chides me for showering twice a day and changing clothes so often, but I just like being clean.

Jared. He'd said he couldn't come. Come where? I feel drugged, my memory fleeting and hard to grasp. I push myself to remember. It was Mom. Mom is sick, she had a stroke. She had probably made it out to be a bigger deal than it is, as she does. She wanted me to come visit, made it seem like she was at death's door, but as we talked, Mom became livelier, dropping the sick act.

So, I drove. Jared and I don't have a lot of money lying around. We're house-poor, but we do alright. We just can't afford plane tickets right now, or at least that's what Jared said. And besides, I remember thinking this then too, Emma would probably hate being on the plane and it would be awful trying fruitlessly to console my poor baby, who's too young to understand altitude, cabin pressure, and her ears needing to pop.

I wanted Jared to come, but he said he was too busy with work. He's always busy with work. He was working on closing a big contract, or something, and couldn't take the time off, he said. There was more to it than that. Jared never liked my mother, but he wouldn't say that was the reason, no, he would only say that he was tied up with work. So, he said he was busy and left me to drive Emma all the way from Richmond, Virginia, to St. Louis, Missouri, a twelve-hour drive if you don't stop. But having a baby, I stopped a lot. These memories flooding in still don't explain how I got here but that's still fuzzy. That woman likely has the answers I need, but I know that isn't happening.

I find I'm able to work my memory forward from the beginning, like I do when trying to find something I've lost. I'll think of the last place I remember using the lost item and go from there. So, I go from the start of my trip. The beginning was mostly uneventful, but something happened while I was cruising through the mountains of West Virginia, or maybe it was Kentucky, while listening to a podcast. Emma had woken up suddenly and was crying, screaming really, so I got off the freeway at the next exit I could find. I had hoped to find a gas station or fast-food restaurant to stop at, but there was nothing. I hadn't thought to check the signs that typically precede highway exits and made a stupid assumption that all exits have *something*. I thought about turning around and getting back on the highway but Emma's cries were becoming unbearable. There was no shoulder on the road I was on, so I found another side street, a scenic tree-lined road. But there was still nowhere to stop, not even a shoulder to pull off onto.

I was about to turn around when I saw the sign saying that there was a scenic vista in about half a mile. I figured that the vista meant there would be at least a small lot for me to park in and tend to Emma. I drove pretty fast down the road, stressed from hearing Emma's ascendingly louder cries for the past fifteen minutes. I nearly made it there before I ran over something which made my tires go immediately flat. A heavy sense of dread filled my heart, but only in retrospect does this feel like it was foreboding. At the time, I was just worried about being stranded in unknown territory.

What did I run over? I remember thinking. I hadn't seen anything in the road, just random drifted piles of dead leaves here and there, which up until then, were fun driving through, hearing them crunch under my tires (in between Emma's screams) and watching them scatter after I passed. But my car rumbled over that last pile and I could both feel and hear that there was something stuck in one, maybe multiple tires. I barely made it to the vista before the car came to rest in the small gravel lot.

Before getting out to check the damage, I first reached between the front seats and unstrapped Emma from her rear-facing car seat to cradle her so she would stop crying. She was dirty, I could smell it. I prioritized Emma's comfort over checking the car's damage, retrieving the diaper bag. I pushed the driver seat back to its full extent, and changed Emma in my lap. Once changed, Emma was again cheerful, smiling up at her favorite person with a gob of drool resting on her lips, making spit bubbles every time she cooed. I smiled back and carried Emma with me as I surveyed the vehicle. As I suspected, both the right-side tires were punctured, with what appeared to be a combination of bone shards and tree limbs. I initially thought they were *human* bones despite being too thin. Seeing the deer antler caught under my rear fender allayed my fears.

I reached into the passenger seat for my cellphone, but found that I had no service. *Those pink maps are bullshit*, I thought, and chucked my phone back in the car. I huffed, rocked Emma, and walked to the view while trying to think of what to do next. Ahead, the terrain sloped down, steeply at first then gently as it reached the valley. Trees peppered with bright fall foliage filled my view. The sun was setting, the sky a deep orange. It was breathtakingly beautiful but I couldn't take in the view as I normally would've liked to do. I needed to find a way out of this predicament. I remember thinking, I could try to pace around until I got a signal. If I could just text someone, maybe they could make the call for me. Also, I wasn't too far from the highway off-ramp, maybe a mile at most. It was walkable, but I didn't really want to walk along a road carrying my baby. So instead, I placed Emma back in her car seat, then got back into the car and sobbed against the steering wheel.

I had given up hope when I heard my phone ping with a Facebook notification. I had service again! Instead of calling roadside assistance, though, I decided to call Jared to give him an update and to have someone to cry to, but my call just went to voicemail. Even when he was in the office, he typically answered my calls and texts. Sometimes when he was super busy, he wouldn't hear the phone ring, he'd said. Our insurance has free roadside assistance, so I called them next, but was placed on hold. After fifteen minutes of being on hold, the call dropped.

I screamed obscenities and gripped my phone as if strangling it, but I refrained from hurling it outside the car window or over the cliff in front of me as I was tempted to do. Instead, I threw it in the diaper bag, where I often keep my things in lieu of a purse since Emma came along. Emma cooed from the backseat, finally happy instead of being restless or upset as she had been almost the entire trip.

I was about to try my insurance company again when I heard the loud grumble of an old pickup truck slowly trundling on the road behind me. *Someone who can help!* I almost jumped out of the car to wave down the truck but thought better of it and started laying onto the horn to get the driver's attention. But the driver had already slowed to stop at the vista before I began honking. The windshield was dirty and cracked, preventing me from seeing who was inside, but I could tell it was just the driver in the cab. The truck stopped next to me and an old, bearded man got out. He was wiry thin and wearing denim overalls with no shirt underneath. "Y'alright, missus?" He spat thickly onto the gravel, having a large wad of tobacco tucked into his lip. "Your tires are all busted up!" He cackled as if it was the funniest thing in the world and spat again.

"Yes, sir," I said, trying to sound polite. "I think I ran over a deer... or at least its remains." I gestured to the tires.

"You sure did." He looked over my tires. "Can't fix that. You'll need new'uns." After spitting again, he said, "there's an auto shop about five miles up the road. They got a tow truck and can sell ya a couple tars." It took me a moment to realize he'd said tires, not tars. "I can give ya a ride if you'd like."

I looked down the empty road. Five miles was a long way to walk with an infant, and what else could I do without a ride from a kind stranger? My cell service seemed to be spotty at best, so my odds of getting a tow truck were certainly slim. "Yeah, sure, thanks. Just give me a minute." I bent over into the backseat to get Emma and heard the old man grunt in approval. *Whatever*, I thought. *All men are pigs, that's a given.* The old man seemed harmless enough. I sized him up after grabbing Emma's diaper bag from the front seat. His thin frame and sagging skin made him look frail. If he did try anything I figured I could overpower him, easily. Until I was about six months pregnant, I used to work out at the gym all the time. Though I still have baby weight, I still feel fit. This didn't stop me from hating the situation. It felt wrong, getting into a truck with a stranger, but what other choice did I have?

He opened the passenger door for me and watched me climb in with another approving grunt, then shut the door behind me. Cradling Emma with my left arm, I buckled the seat belt, which only covered my waist which I attributed to the antiquity of the truck. I hugged Emma to my chest, the best alternative I could manage to an infant car seat.

The truck pulled out of the vista parking lot and I watched my car disappear as we moved away. Probably because of my stress, it took me a few minutes to notice that the old man had guided the truck further down the tree-lined road, not back to the main road I had come from. I assumed that when he'd said that the shop was five miles away that it must be off the main road, but then I thought maybe he meant that it was in this direction. *Maybe he knows a shortcut.* Dusk was approaching quickly, the trees' long shadows filling the road. The old man had the radio set to a country music station which I didn't care for but I didn't say anything, not wanting to be rude.

Soon, the truck was barreling down the road, moving too fast for my comfort, especially since I was cradling Emma. I wouldn't have thought that such a relic would be capable of moving this fast. I held Emma tighter.

"Cute baby," the old man said.

"Thank you," I whispered.

"How old is it?" He looked away from the road briefly to eye Emma.

"*She's* about three months old."

He whistled. "You look good for just havin' a baby only a few months ago. Real sexy." He reached over and squeezed my thigh with his bony fingers.

My shock at the audacity and surprise of the action delayed my response. I moved my leg away, though he'd already moved his hand. "Um, please don't touch me."

"Oh, don't be a bitch," the old man said.

My mouth dropped open. "Excuse me?" Before I could say anything else, a dirty, wet cloth was forcefully covering my mouth and nose. It smelled like bleach. Most confusing of all was that the old man still had both hands on the wheel. He had started joyfully singing along off-tune to the country music, tapping his hands on the steering wheel off-beat. I tried to wrench my head away from whoever or whatever was holding the cloth to my head, but whoever was holding me back was strong.

As my vision began to fade, I felt the old man squeeze my thigh again. I heard him say, "Night-night, bitch."

2

Daniel

What I expected was that the steel would taste like steel. Instead, I can taste the thin layer of oil on the barrel of the gun, an industrial, machine sort of taste, with a hint of orange rinds. I savor the gun in my mouth like it's my last meal, and in a way, it is. I close my eyes and pull on the trigger. *Clack.*

The hammer's loud click causes me to flinch. I gently place the gun back on the table and pour another shot of whiskey which I down with a grimace. After lifting the revolver again, I spin the chamber a few times and pull back the hammer. This is the second night I've played this game. This morning, I was completely flummoxed after having fallen asleep from overdrinking. It didn't make sense that I could spin the chamber more than a dozen times and never land on the bullet inside. It seemed impossible. *No, impossible would be the same thing happening two nights in a row.*

I began playing this game shortly after I got the cancer diagnosis. Months ago, I'd gone into the local Urgent Care clinic when the migraines started becoming frequent and unbearable. The doctor asked about my water intake (minimal), exercise level (nonexistent), diet (terrible), and alcohol consumption (at the time, not much, truly). I'd made an effort because the headaches were awful, but none of my lifestyle changes seemed to help, and on top of the headaches, I'd started having tremors. I thought they were seizures until the doctor told me that with seizures, you don't remember anything that happens during them. Still, the doctor recommended a CT scan, which I learned was just an x-ray of my brain. That's how they found the dark spot which ended up being a Stage 3 brain tumor. It was midbrain so it would be a difficult and expensive operation. Not to mention the costly remediation, chemotherapy, doctor's appointments, and a partridge in a pear tree. I would never be able to afford any of that, so I either would live out the remainder of my days in relative comfort, ignoring the headaches which I could tame with enough Advil, or rack up medical bills for a treatment that isn't guaranteed to work and would leave me bald, sickly, and broke, probably homeless.

I made the mistake of telling my mom about the diagnosis, but in lieu of taking money out of Dad's retirement fund to pay for the treatment I needed, she started a prayer circle at her church. They all laid a hand on me for healing, with another hand up, pointed at the Almighty, the official Evangelical Christian salute. God didn't heal me, but the offering they collected allowed me to buy a Smith & Wesson revolver and ammunition from a local pawn shop. The box of rounds was dusty and probably too old to work which may explain my current predicament of the gun not doing its fucking job and killing me. The money also got me a 1.5-liter bottle of Jack Daniels. "It has your name on it!" the clerk had said with a sneer after reading my license. *Daniel, Daniels, right.* I figure if I have to die soon, I might as well go out with a bang, so to speak. Plus, the icing on the cake will be that the landlord will have to pay someone to clean chunks of my cancer-ridden brain from the cheap, brittle apartment carpet, and considering how often he pounds on the door at seven in the morning just because I forgot to pay the rent on the exact day its due, despite there being a five-day grace period per the leasing agreement, it won't hurt to cause the asshole an added inconvenience.

Reminiscing on the ridiculousness of the prayer circle, I set down the revolver to pour a bonus shot, a toast to dogma. I pour the shot, kill it, and lift the revolver to my lips, the hammer still drawn. I close my eyes and am about to pull the trigger when my phone rings, causing me to drop the revolver which misfires when it hits the floor, the round blasting through the window and into the night sky. Coincidentally, that window is open, mostly because the AC sucks, so the only damage to the apartment is a small hole in the window screen. I blink and fish the phone out from my pocket. It's Ben. He and I have been lifelong friends and were roommates before Ben joined the Army and went on two deployments to Afghanistan.

"Oh Danny Boy, the pipes, the pipes are calling," Ben croons when I pick up.

I add an easygoing perkiness to my voice which I'm not feeling. "Hey, man, what's up? I thought you were still in Afghanistan."

"Nah, I got back a few weeks ago. Sorry for not calling sooner, I've been pretty fucking busy. You'll never believe it. I'm finally done! I'm getting out!"

"Oh nice! So, when are you getting back to Virginia?" I pace around the living room, away from the bottle of Jack and the gun on the floor.

"That's actually what I'm calling about. How would you like to have a road trip, just like old times?" Soon after we'd gotten our driver's licenses, we made it a near-monthly habit to drive off in a random direction, often with no destination in mind. At one point, we even went to Burger King, back when they had a spinning wheel you could flick to help decide what combo to get, and used their wheel as a compass, flicking it to decide which direction to travel. "I need to get my car back home and I figured this would be a fun way to do it. Look, I sign my papers in a few days, which is short notice, I know, but apparently, I have way more terminal leave saved up than I thought." Ben clears his throat. "So, Danny Boy, do you think you could swing it? And before you say anything, don't worry about the cost of the plane ticket to get here. I got a *bunch* of money dumped in my account from the Army, some kind of delayed payment on my reenlistment bonus from a few years back. Tax-free, too. So, I'm *flushed with cash*." Ben sings the last few words in a high falsetto.

I look back to the revolver on the floor, then to the phone. Ben's picture in the phone is from the sixth grade when he had that embarrassing bowl cut. "Yeah. Yeah, I'm in. Let's do it."

"Let's fuckin' goooooo!" Ben screams into the phone and I pull it away from my ear. I hate that phrase and how it has strangely fallen into every dude-bro's vernacular, but forgive Ben this one trespass.

We talk out the details. I'll fly out to Seattle, the closest airport to Fort Lewis, which is just south of Tacoma, where Ben is currently stationed. We estimate the trip will take five or six days, depending on how frequently we stop, if we happen upon any roadside attractions that catch our interest. For the first time since the diagnosis, I think of something other than doom and gloom.

I go to bed with a plan to cancel the apartment lease in the morning. I really don't want to live here anymore and hate the idea of continuing to pay for a place I detest, especially if I'm going to be gone for a week or longer of the next rented month.

After packing what I want to keep in a duffel bag, I sell what I can through the same pawn shop which sold me the gun —the TV for forty bucks and the couch for twenty—then donate what I know they won't take to Goodwill, though in retrospect it would have been far easier to just toss it all in the apartment complex's dumpster.

As promised, Ben buys the plane ticket, so I just have to front the cost of the Uber to get to the airport. I turn in the key before I leave and am promised the prorated rent back for the month, as well as the last month's rent and deposit I paid at the start of the lease, less any damages. I give my mom's house as the mailing address for this repayment check, should it ever arrive. *Damages,* I think laughingly. I consider the near miss with the bullet going out the window and what the landlord would have thought of a bullet hole in the wall had the revolver fired in another direction.

I keep the gun, so will have to check the duffel with the airline. I just don't want to get rid of this escape rope from what is an inevitably painful end to my miserable life. I don't tell anyone else I'm leaving, not that anyone would care. I don't have a job since I quit shortly after the diagnosis. My *career* as a line cook at Applebee's with its no health insurance nor paid leave wasn't really doing me any favors with my exciting new cancer journey.

Now I have something to look forward to. While packing and clearing out the apartment, I discover the credit card I'd opened years ago and never thought to close. It has a zero balance and a $5,000 credit limit, so it will be a ton of free money for the trip. Capitol One can't send their goons after a dead man, and this way I won't feel guilty about Ben paying for everything on the trip with his money. We can have fun and I can put off thinking about my mortality for the time being. I won't be able to forget the cancer, not with the frequent migraines, but alcohol and painkillers dulls the pain enough to be tolerable so that's something.

When I get to the airport, I realize I haven't flown in a very long time. It almost feels foreign. I get to the airport four hours in advance, too early to even check my bag, so I have to wait in the lobby for an hour. Because of the gun, I'm nervous, as if I'm a teenager with a fake ID trying to buy beer, though there's no complications. Once past security, I buy a souvenir from the Hudson News store, a small snow globe with the Richmond skyline as a gift for Ben, as well as a large bottle of water and a paperback to read on the plane.

Once in the air, I order several Jack and Cokes, hoping to numb myself. I'm not scared of the plane crashing, as some may be—I don't fear death, and in fact a plane crash would come as a blessing. No, another one of my migraines is coming on strong and the cabin pressure is only making it worse. Much worse. I feel like my head is going to explode. I've taken about a dozen 200mg Advil, along with multiple drinks—though the flight attendants haven't cut me off and instead happily slide the credit card—but the massive migraine doesn't seem to want to abate. It only goes away once the plane has landed, and even then, its ghost lingers.

When Ben greets me at Seattle-Tacoma International, he's carrying a neon pink glittery poster with my name in red paint, the I dotted with a heart. The sign has to be more embarrassing for Ben to carry than it is for me to approach him. I just laugh appreciably and give him a hug. I retrieve my checked duffel which bears a tag indicating it's been inspected by TSA, likely due to the gun showing up on their x-ray. I googled the regulations and carefully complied with them—it's in a hard case (the one it came with) and I'd ensured it was clear of ammunition. The one round that *had* been it went through the window a couple nights ago. I'm suddenly worried they seized the gun despite following all of their rules, so I unzip the duffel and check inside. It's still there.

Ben rolls up the glittery poster and stuffs it into a nearby trashcan as we make our way to the parking lot. We begin our trip by heading to Seattle proper since I haven't been there before. We walk to the Space Needle, but decide not to deal with the line to get inside. We go to the fish market, but at the time, they aren't doing the famous fish toss, so there isn't much to see. We get coffee at the first Starbucks. We walk by the Fremont Troll, an eighteen-foot-tall concrete statue surrounded by sleeping homeless people. When we get back to Ben's car, it has a parking ticket on it for staying past the three-hour limit.

Tired from walking, we pass through Portland without stopping, and get a hotel in Southern Oregon. Despite the day being long and the drive uneventful, I never find the opportunity to bring up the cancer diagnosis. No, that's not true, I have to admit. There were certainly opportunities on the eight or so hours that we drove, filled with music and mixed conversation. I just couldn't bring myself to do it.

For the next several days, we stop for a few hours here and there. We stop in Winnemucca, Nevada, where the signs proclaim we will "Win big in Winnemucca!" We don't win big, but we do get plenty wasted from free drinks while playing video poker at the bar for a quarter per play. When Ben drinks, I'm treated to a heavy helping of Ben's PTSD from his tours in Afghanistan, a quick aggressiveness and general dickish attitude which only peeks out from time to time when Ben is sober but really rears its ugly head while he's drunk. We almost fight when I make a joke that night and Ben doesn't take it well.

On the last night of the trip, we stay in a hotel in Louisville, Kentucky, about nine hours away from Chesterfield, Virginia, where our 3,500-mile road trip will come to an end. By this point, I decide to tell Ben about the brain tumor after the trip is over, or maybe the next day. It's a wonder, really, that he hasn't asked any questions when I've been eating about twenty Advil per day. My anxiety about telling him doesn't help me sleep, so end up getting drunk in the hotel room and passing out.

3

Sam

I've rubbed my wrists raw trying to wriggle them out of the rope restraints. I tried pulling at them, but this only seems to make the knots tighter. The ropes are old and frayed, so I thought with enough force, I'd be able to snap them off, but I only end up hurting myself.

I can't remember if I had anything useful in my pockets, not that it matters now since I have no idea where my clothes are. I'm completely naked, lying in a drying puddle of my own urine. This is the worst. I called for that woman to come let me use the restroom, but she didn't hear me, or plainly ignored me, so I ended up pissing myself again, further soaking the mattress.

I can hear a television blaring from the other room, what sounds like cartoons, likely for the benefit of Emma. I didn't want my baby exposed to screens, at least not until she's six years old or so. I've seen those zombie-like children in shopping cart seats at the grocery store, or at restaurants, faces lit by iPads two inches from their eyes, playing Cocomelon or Blippi or some mindless app. I don't want that life for my Emma, but now here I am being thankful for the cartoons because at least it means that Emma is probably safe. Hopefully the cartoons aren't violent.

Based on my memory of events, the old man must have taken me here, and there must have been someone else in the truck with him, though where they had been, I have no clue. This wasn't a modern truck with a large dual-cab, it was ancient. There is no way someone else was in the vehicle with us, and yet there must have been.

Feeding Emma has made me sleepy, but I try to force myself to stay awake. I don't want to be caught unaware should someone come in, not that I can do anything with my wrists and ankles tied to the bed. I can barely move my elbows and knees, the restraints are so tight. I lift my head and look around the room, though now the room is dark. When that woman had left last time, she'd turned off the overhead light, leaving me in darkness. My eyes have adjusted to the dark, but this doesn't offer much assistance. With nothing else left to do, I fall asleep.

An indeterminate amount of time later, I wake to the light being cut back on, blindingly. I see the shape of the woman, again carrying a crying Emma. "Wake up, bitch, she's hungry again." and she presses Emma's face against my right breast.

"Please," I say, "tell me why I'm here."

"Why does that even matter? It won't help you none," says the young woman, lighting up a cigarette and plopping herself back down on the chair. She's topless and wearing panties which is more than I can say for myself. She must have gotten up from bed to the baby crying then taken her in here after changing her and soothing her didn't work. "Ugh, you smell like piss."

"What do you expect?" I say through my teeth. The woman only smiles in response, that same shit-eating grin. "Can you at least put her on my left breast? It's becoming engorged. It really hurts."

She looks over at my other breast and says, "Oh, you ain't kidding! You know what, I know just the thing that'll help!" She leaves the room. Emma remains balanced on my chest, tethered only by her own suction. I wish I could crane my neck to kiss her, but I'm afraid that any movement would cause Emma to roll off and fall onto the floor. The best I can do is sniff hard to take in her scent. I relish it.

The blonde comes back in, wearing her now typical cat-who-ate-the-canary grin, and goes back to her chair. Before I can ask her anything, someone else enters. It's the old man from the truck. It takes me a moment to recognize him since I've only seen him once before, and at the time he was wearing oil-stained denim overalls. Now, he's stripped down to yellowed briefs. His arms are thin but his torso is pudgy and loose with a flabby gut hanging over the worn strap of his underwear. His chest and arms are speckled with liver spots which extend to his neck.

"Krystal tells me you need some help." The old man gives a toothless grin and struts over to the bedside. He walks like he's coming over to repair a busted pipe. *Was he toothless before?* I can't remember. The old man crouches by the left side of the bed, the side closest to the door, with a groan, his knees popping loudly in succession. *Pop, pop!* With one cold, gnarled hand, he cups my left breast, leans in, and pops my nipple in his mouth.

A whimpering "No..." is all I can manage and my vision begins to swim from revulsion. I feel as though vomiting is imminent. Afraid I will puke all over Emma, or worse, choke on my own upchuck, with watering eyes I swallow a mouthful of acid that has come up my throat. I very much would like to push the elderly man off of my breast, but my hands are bound, and I can do nothing to jerk away or buck him off without risking throwing Emma to the floor. I'm stuck. I have to refrain from all movement while the disgusting old man gleefully drinks from me. I can feel the milk let down in my left breast as the old man suckles on it, drinking greedily. With his hand still on my breast, he squeezes gently at first, then roughly, expressing more and more milk into his waiting mouth.

I normally get a warming pleasure from nursing Emma. I feel this joy even when it sometimes hurts a bit from having sore, chapped nipples. I find no pleasure this time, as my entire focus is on trying (and failing) to ignore the disgusting old man using me for sustenance, or worse, pleasure. With my limited movement and current field of view, it's impossible to completely shut him out, aside from closing my eyes. But I also don't want to miss this fleeting moment of being able to see Emma. To make matters worse, the old man is looking up to me while sucking on my nipple, sickeningly reminding me of how Emma looks up at me with her big crossed eyes, wonderingly, while feeding. His eyes are fixed though, gauging my reaction, as if hoping I'm enjoying this act as much as he.

With his lips and slimy tongue, he pulls my entire areola into his toothless mouth. He sucks my nipple hard, agonizingly. My nipples have become much more sensitive since Emma's birth, thanks to near-constant feeding. I can feel my nipple draw into the old man's mouth with each suck, and then pop out to his gums, but not all the way out of his mouth before it sucks back in. His mouth feels slimy. He loudly gulps the milk down, his Adam's apple bobbing against my ribs. He breathes hard through his nose as he sucks.

"Woo wee!" the old man exclaims after unlatching. With great effort, he brings himself back into a standing position. He looks at me with a gleam in his eye as he cartoonishly laps his tongue around his lips then uses the back of his hand to wipe the drool and excess milk from his mouth and chin. "Now that,... that was the best milk I mighta had in my whole life!"

With him standing, I can see that his penis is hard through his briefs. There's a drop of moisture dotting the end of where I can see his dick pushing against the fabric. I scream at him, which causes him to startle, then burst into laughter. He gives my left breast a playful but painful slap, then leaves the room with a dismissive wave in my direction. "'Til next time, bitch!"

The blonde—Krystal is her name, I've learned—scoops up a milk-drunk Emma and leaves directly behind him, saying "Sleep tight! Don't let the bed bugs bite!" She turns off the light as she exits, and locks all four locks on the door behind her.

I scream after them, "What is wrong with you people?" before breaking into sobs.

The house once again grows quiet. The room becomes overpowered by the frogs and other noisemaking wildlife outside. I know I have to a find a way out of this mess, but everything I come up with requires outside assistance, someone coming to rescue us. Feeling helpless and alone, I eventually fall back to sleep.

4

Krystal

I finally got me my own baby! I been wantin' one for a coupla years now, but ain't no man good enough to put their seed in me. Didn't wanna deal with some daddy anyhow, just wanted a baby all my own and then the other day the Good Lord answered my prayers and gave me a baby! What an early Christmas surprise too!

I'm just settin' around watchin' my soaps when my phone goes off. I know, it don't make no sense that a redneck girl like myself got a cell phone and one of them smart phones no less! Well, I'll have you know you need one nowadays! And they come cheap if you know how to get them at the 7-Eleven downtown. You just buy one of them cards and you can put minutes on it and still get the fancy apps and everything. Anyway, Grandaddy was the one who got the cameras at Wal-Mart and he set me to read the instructions and set it up so we know when one goes off. They're cellular trail cams and while I was readin' the instructions, which takes me all damn day mind you, I realize I need a smart phone to set it up. Otherwise, we'd have no idea if we done caught us a bunny unless we drive 'round all day, every day, and what the hell fun is that? So, like I said, I'm watchin' my soaps and my phone goes off and I look at it right away, and what do you know, some lady done plowed right through the trap that's only about ten minutes down the road. We been doing the traps long as I can remember, prob'ly since before I was even born. The deer bones were Grandaddy's idea, much better than anything else. I mean if the police find the bones on the road or if somebody runs over it and we can't get to them in time before the tow truck comes or somebody else comes to help 'em, they wouldn't think nothin' of it. For all they know, some cougar or bear was draggin' a carcass down the road and got scared off by a car.

So, me and Grandaddy hop in his old pickup, me hidin' behind the seat. We keep a mason jar with some homemade chloroform back there so we don't need to grab nothin'. Did you know you can make chloroform with just some bleach and acetone? It's real easy. Grandaddy is real good at it, too, but he can make a mean moonshine and it about amounts to the same thing if you ask me. So, we pull up on the ol' Damsel in Distress who turns out to be a real whiny bitch, but what we come to find out is that she has a little one. And Grandaddy did say last year that if we ever caught somebody with a baby that I could keep it for my own! I hear her get in the truck and I sit real still so she don't hear me and don't realize I'm in there too. Grandaddy's keepin' real quiet at first too. I unscrew the lid of that jar real quiet and get the rag ready on top. It don't take me but a minute and Grandaddy's truck's so loud you can't hear nothin' anyway. Then he says, "Cute baby," and I swear to God my heart leaps out my chest when he says that. I'm so excited I wanna scream! Mind, I'm hidin' everything including my head behind that seat and the baby ain't makin' no noise so I ain't had no clue the bunny had a lil' baby with her! They say something else, I don't know what. I'm just waitin' for Grandaddy to call her a bitch. Once he calls the bunnies a name, that's when I know the truck is going too fast for her to jump out, not that she would with that baby but still I want to do this right. So, he calls her a bitch and I jump up with the rag and shove it over her mouth so quick she ain't got time to see me. I'm real lucky I don't hit the baby in the head since she's holding it up so high, but that woulda been her fault not mine! It don't take long for her to pass out and Grandaddy pulls over so I can get up front. We put the bunny in the back and I get to carry the baby, and I swear it's gotta be a sign because she looks just like me! She's got my eyes and everything!

Before we go on back home, Grandaddy pulls the truck around so we can take care of the bunny's car. I put on my dish gloves and go through the car lookin' for somethin' worth keepin and there ain't nothin' 'cept a pair of sunglasses. Grandaddy takes down the rails from the fence in front of her car. It's just a split-rail. And I put the car in neutral. Me and Grandaddy push the car to the edge and let it roll down the hill, and it makes it pretty far down before we hear the crunch of it hittin' a tree or maybe another car. This ain't the first time this trap's got us a bunny! I help Grandaddy put the fence back together and we head on.

I take the baby in the house first thing. We still have the crib from when I was a baby, but it's full of random shit so I have to put her on the couch until we get everything else done. So, I go fetch Big Joe. He's my brother but he's simple so he don't come out to fetch the bunnies with us, 'cause he wouldn't be smart enough to play along. He just stays home, jerks off, and watches cartoons, sometimes all at the same time. I've definitely walked in on him pullin' his pud more times than I care to count! He don't stop though, he just keeps on goin' like he don't mind his sister walkin' in on him jerkin' off! Anyway, Big Joe's just nappin' when I go to fetch him this time, so he's a bit pissy but he listens because he don't want Grandaddy to get the switch. We tie the bunny up in the Bunny Room, which Grandaddy says used to be my Momma and Daddy's room before they died. I don't remember them since they died so long ago. The bunny's still asleep so we strip off her clothes and rope her up, then leave her be, givin' me time to make room for my new baby. I don't know what the bunny lady calls her but she's so tiny there ain't no way the baby knows her name yet. So that means I can come up with a name for her! I'm thinkin' Jolene like the Dolly Parton song and it's such a pretty name. I don't know, I got some time to think it over. The problem with not having a Momma around is you don't know the first thing about takin' care of a baby 'cept what you get from the TV. I have to look it up on the Internet using my phone like everything else it seems and it don't seem too hard really. You just gotta keep their diaper clean and their belly full, and that's about it. Of course, there's the lovin' part but that comes easy! I love my new baby girl, she's perfect! Feedin' her's another thing since we ain't got no formula, so we gotta use the bunny for the time bein'. How it goes the first day, is if I can't get the baby to shut up from changing her diaper or walking her around, and I'm fixin' to get a real bad headache from all the cryin', I just take her to the bunny and put her to titty. I was doing just that and last night the bitch has the gall to tell me to put my baby on her *other* titty because her titty hurts or something, saying that her titties are gettin' engorged like I don't know what that means. Funny enough, Grandaddy just said at dinner that he'd like to suck on one of them titties and drink all the milk when I was complaining that we needed to pick up some formula so we wouldn't have to rely on the bunny. He said formula's expensive, more expensive than feeding an adult, so we just have to deal with having the bitch around until the baby is eating real people food. I think he mighta been looking for an excuse to keep her around for a bit longer so he can suck her titties and fuck her. So yeah, I go and fetch Grandaddy because I'm tired of the bitch's bitching (ha, ha) and I thought I'd get a real kick out of watching her face while Grandaddy drinks from her. And you know what, I do! She hates it! Then right after I put the baby back down to sleep again, my phone goes off. It's another bunny! Normally we take down all the traps after we catch us a bunny, but this time we ain't had the chance yet, what with the girl bunny and my new baby. Normally we don't catch more than one car worth of bunnies each year because we don't want there to be too many people goin' missin' all at the same time. Folks might start lookin' a little too close to home. So, I go in to wake Grandaddy up, but he won't asleep yet. I think he's jerking off thinking about sucking on that bitch's titty. Anyway, he acts like he won't doin' nothin' and hops to it. "We got enough room," he says and throws on his overalls. He's got sweat all over his forehead so I know he musta been jerkin' off. This one was Trap Number 3 which is about an hour away from our house. I feel bad leavin' the baby by herself for a few hours but I figure she'd be fine having just been fed and all. It don't take long before I end up fallin' asleep in the truck even though I'm squished up behind the seat! Grandaddy wakes me up with a quick tap before gettin' out the car to talk to the next bunny. I can't wait to see what we caught! What if it's another baby?

5

Daniel

We sleep through our alarms and wake at about 10:30, just half an hour before we have to check out, else pay for another night. The blackout curtains did not help us get up in time. We scramble to gather our belongings and stuff them in our respective bags. Then we miss the hotel's free continental breakfast by sleeping in, so have to stop by a nearby diner for some greasy breakfast and bitter coffee.

This is the last day, I think while eating. I have to tell Ben, if no one else, about the diagnosis. It isn't that I don't think Ben can handle the information. Truly, I'm more worried Ben will try to pay for my medical care, spend all of the money the military gave him for re-enlisting a few years back, which is bullshit. Why should Ben waste all of his money which could be spent on something more worthwhile when there's no way to even know if the treatments would do anything? They might not even extend my life at all, just make it so I feel deathly ill and poisoned for my last few months. I suppose that's why I didn't press my parents to donate their retirement fund for my treatment, as it's essentially the same thing. They saved up that money for decades so that my dad can retire soon. What a waste to spend it on quickening my death, if that's what comes of it.

Now I'm anxious, faced with the looming end of our trip, when I promised myself that I would reveal all. I can't *not* tell Ben. There is no getting out of my end, so Ben will certainly find out eventually, and to not be told beforehand, he would feel betrayed. That's not how I want to leave things with him, even though things have been fairly rocky on this trip thanks to Ben's PTSD.

Now that we're closer to home, Ben starts asking me about mutual acquaintances, how they are doing, what they are up to now. This conversation dies off after it is obvious that my answer to every question is a variation of "I'm not sure," "I haven't talked to him/her in a while," or "let me check Facebook." It's only too perfect I've been presented with a life-threatening disease after decidedly ostracizing myself from everyone around me. I can't even pinpoint what led to this voluntary self-exclusion. It started with turning down invites to the bar, mostly for monetary reasons, but also because I got tired of the same old conversations. I was even tired of fucking friends and then trying to pretend like nothing had happened the next day, neither party permitted to bring it up.

We made it three thousand miles without incident, aside from the parking ticket in Seattle, so it is no surprise when we run over something in the mountains of West Virginia while singing loudly to "Bohemian Rhapsody." We were overdue for something to happen, really. Although Ben is driving at the time, I'm not completely blameless for the incident, as it is me who needed to make an emergency bathroom stop, causing us to leave Interstate 64 for the less populated and more heavily wooded areas of the mountainous state. We absconded with a roll of toilet paper from the first hotel we stayed in, so we're ready for such an emergency. Plus, I get to tell Ben about how I made the mistake of shitting with my ass pointing *up* the hill, forcing me to have to duckwalk away from liquid shit running down the hill chasing me. With anyone else, this story would be embarrassing, but with Ben, it's just funny.

Whatever Ben runs over causes at least one of his tires to become flat almost immediately. We both have experienced flat tires before. What we're used to though is the standard flat tire which occurs when you run over something like a screw and it feels like running over a small rock. You might hear the tap-tap-

tap-tap of the screw head hitting the road while your tire rolls on the pavement. And if you turn down the radio, you might even hear the steady hiss of the air leaving the tire. Instead of that, Ben's tire suddenly bursts, causing the car to jerk to the right, going immediately into the ditch, which is deep enough to rub the car's undercarriage on the thin, gravel shoulder. I don't look back, but I'm sure sparks fly behind us as the metal scrapes rock. Even though every driving school in America advises against it, Ben's first reaction is to overcorrect, pushing the car quickly back to the left, which causes both right-side tires to leave the road and my side of the car to become airborne. If I hadn't just shit on the mountainside, I would have filled my pants just now. The car slams back down, popping the remaining right-side tire. Ben pounds his foot on the brakes to prevent any further chaos and puts the car in park.

"Well, that was fun," I say flatly.

"Yyyyep," Ben responds in a similar monotone. The car is in the center of the two-lane road, but no cars are coming and there isn't much of a shoulder anyway, so Ben doesn't make an effort to pull the car over. Without a word, we both unbuckle and get out to inspect the damage. I nearly trip as I'm not ready for how low my side of the car is. Ben walks over and curses under his breath. "Well, I have a donut we can use," he says pointing to his trunk, indicating the spare tire, "for *one* of the busted tires, but that doesn't really help us in this situation."

"We'll have to call a tow truck." I pull out my phone. It's dead. I had forgotten to plug it in at the hotel overnight and also hadn't thought to charge it on the drive. I am clearly too preoccupied with having to tell another person about the poison eating away at my brain. "My phone's dead apparently. You'll have to use yours."

Ben reaches in through the passenger side to pull his phone off the dash. It was mounted there so we could use it for GPS. When he pulls it out, the GPS application's map is empty.

There isn't even a road on the display. The little cartoon car sits in an all-white void. Small text above where the map should be indicates that the application is having difficulty obtaining both network access and GPS connection. In place of where his phone shows his connectivity as ascending bars, there is simply an X next to the antenna icon. "Well, this sucks," he says. "I've got no service."

I look in both directions of the road, as if through will alone I can cause a passing motorist to approach, to help us out, but I can't even hear the cars from the freeway. We've gone too far. "This is a paved road. Cars have to come by at some point, right? Our only other option would be to walk back toward the freeway until we see someone."

Ben is looking up the wooded hill, which may be a small mountain. "Or I could walk up there and see if I get service. Might be quicker that way."

I also look up the incline but can't see an end to the climb. "Are you sure it's quicker? It might not even work up there."

"It's worth a try. How about this – you try your way, I'll try mine. That way, no time is wasted and we'll make sure we get out of here before it gets dark." It's already starting to get dark, thanks to the shorter fall days.

"Alright," I say hesitantly. It feels weird leaving the car unattended, but Ben is also right that there isn't really a guarantee that either idea will work, which he implied by wanting to try both ideas. Ben is in great physical condition from the Army, having lugged around bags on ruck marches, so climbing the hill unencumbered is nothing to him. I watch him walk up until he disappears behind a large bush at the base of some trees.

I start walking back in the direction from which we came. There is no telling what lies ahead of the car, and my vague sense of direction could lead me back to the freeway, so that is the safest bet. Unfortunately, with my phone completely dead, there would be no way for me to tell Ben if I find someone. I'll just have to hope we meet back up at the car. Without a phone or watch, I also have no sense of time in how long I've been walking. The road seems to go on for a long while, probably miles. We pulled down this road so that I could shit, and then continued in the same direction looking for a turnoff or a place to pull a U-y before Ben had run over whatever that was on the road. It looked sort of like bones, but it was hard to say. We were more focused on how much of an issue we're dealing with, without considering the cause.

It feels like it's been about twenty minutes of walking, though it could have been ten, when I come to the pile of leaves that we had run over, and sure enough, there are pieces of what look to be bones in the road. I kick the leaves around to reveal a deer skull, which I assume to be a doe based on the lack of antlers. It seems odd that there are just bones in the road, not a deer's body or carcass. Only the bones. *How is this possible?* I think. The deer may have been hit by a car long enough ago that it decomposed on the road, then no one else did anything about it. This would explain why all of the bones seem shattered. In fact, they are all spikes, certainly capable of piercing a tire. It seems like too many coincidences, but then again, this road isn't very well traveled, so it all is possible. I don't like the idea of some hapless motorist, maybe the one who can get us out of this jam, coming along and hitting the same road hazard, making themselves also in need of a tow truck and incapable of helping us, so I kick the bones over to the shoulder and into the ditch as much as I can.

Just as I finish, I hear a small click come from the direction of the woods. I swear it sounded like a camera shutter snapping, but this doesn't make sense. It must have been an acorn falling, or a squirrel snapping a twig. I continue down the road.

It takes what feels like more than half an hour to come in sight of the crossroad. It's dusk, and the trees on both sides make the road even darker. At least I can periodically hear cars driving by on the freeway, so I know I'm close, and I know there will be a chance of flagging someone down. I can't see the highway though, since it's blocked by another tree line and probably a slope down if I correctly recall the offramp's incline. This presents me with two options: I can stay here at the main road, if you could call it that, and hope to flag someone down, or I can walk all the way back to the offramp to flag someone down. The odds of finding someone at this intersection are probably better than if I had stayed by the car, but without a car in sight, who knows how long I would have to wait. The bright side would be that it would be easier to flag someone down here, should I see a car approaching, since they would be going much slower than the nearby Interstate. Obviously, the freeway has a relatively regular amount of traffic, ensuring *someone* will see me, but they would be not only less able to stop but also likely less willing to pull over for some strange man on the side of the freeway. There is the third option of just walking back to the car and admitting that maybe Ben was right that climbing the mountain was the better of the two ideas. If my phone had a charge, I would have at least been able to check to see if I have service now that I'm in a more open area.

Walking back isn't really a good idea. If Ben is able to get connectivity wherever he has climbed, the tow truck would likely have to pass by me before it gets to Ben's car. I could flag it down most likely, or if not, could walk back when the tow truck passes. If Ben *isn't* able to get service at the top of the hill, walking back would be just a waste of time since we would then have to hoof it back to where I am now. It also doesn't make sense to simply stand at the intersection waiting for a car. If there is a car on this road, I can flag it down while I'm walking, so really, heading back to the offramp is exercising both of the better choices.

I spend so long deliberating over the multiple choice test I have in front of me, as I stare off vacantly, that I almost don't notice the pickup approaching, even though it is very noisy. I begin to wave it down, but I am apprehensive about it being able to stop because it is almost literally flying down the road. But it's already slowing down before it gets to me, so the driver must have seen me before I even signaled. Nonetheless, I wave.

6

Krystal

Grandaddy gets out of the truck and starts talking to this young-soundin' man on the side of the road. They're right outside the truck so I can just about hear everything they say.

The boy bunny says, "Thanks for stopping. Me and my friend ran over some debris on the side road behind me, maybe half a mile down. At least two of our tires are completely busted and we've having a hard time getting service."

"Oh yeah?" Grandaddy says, playing dumb. "Is your friend still by your car?"

"Yeah, well, I mean he might be. He walked up the hill to try to get service, I'm not sure if he's made his way back down yet."

Grandaddy laughs. "I s'pose he's gonna hafta give up some time! There's still trees at the top of that mountain, so service ain't much better! He'd be better off walking down the road like you did!" The boy bunny is quiet for a minute. I'm hoping he doesn't realize how familiar Grandaddy seems with this particular stretch of road and its level of cellular service. "You know, there's a tow company about five minutes up the road that away, but they close in about fifteen minutes. I could take you back to your car and see if your friend made his way back over there, but we might not make it to the tow place in time."

"No, let's go to the tow company first. We can go back after."

"Alrighty," Grandaddy says and I hear him jump in the

truck.

Next, I hear the bunny get in the truck. There ain't no tow truck company for probably fifty miles, but Grandaddy's smarter than he lets on. Course this ain't the first time we done this neither. He needs the bunny to think we got a good reason to be flying down the road in the wrong direction as his car. He also knows he ain't got long before the bunny would get suspicious.

"So, you and your friend," Grandaddy says. "You two a coupla' faggots?"

"What the fuck did you just say?" And I shut the bunny up. I pop up like a jack in the box with the ol' rag and throw it on his face. He's strong though and bucks against me, even grabbin' on my hands, tryin' to pull me off him. But I'm pretty strong myself and can hold my own. Before you know it, he goes limp under me, but I keep on holdin' it on him. I don't want him playing possum and springing up on me like Freddy Krueger or Jason.

"Alright, that's enough," Grandaddy says, pulling the truck over. I'm a little surprised to see that the bunny is a black boy, since he didn't really sound like one. He's definitely heavier than the last bunny, the girl bunny with the baby, so it takes a bit of grunting to get him in the bed of the pickup. Grandaddy throws the tarp over him and a coupla bricks to hold the tarp down, then we're headin' back around to the trap.

Before long, we're stopped again. Grandaddy's outta the pickup and talkin' to another boy bunny. I can't hear 'em talkin' as much this time, but it all ends the same. The bunny gets in the truck and even buckles up like a good little boy. My guess is Grandaddy told him they could look for his friend. This time I really douse the rag, really soak it good with the homemade chloroform. I don't wanna take no chances. When Grandaddy calls the bunny a faggot like the other one, I pop on up and get him with the rag. I must've done the rag right, 'cause he falls right to sleep.

When we get to their car, we see there won't be no movin'

it this time. This is one of our older traps, so I'm surprised the camera's battery still works. Plus, the reception sucks out here, something we learned to do better about, so I'm also surprised the camera is able to send us pictures. Usually, it only works in the daytime, Lord knows why. We don't have much time to root around their car, so we just grab the duffel bags we find in the trunk, throw bunny boy number two in the bed, grab the camera so we can it put it up somewhere else next year, and head on home. Normally we leave the camera up, but this one has got such bad coverage, plus we're leavin' the car here, so Grandaddy says to get it. This might be the fastest we caught two cars' worth of bunnies for the winter! We should be eatin' good tomorrow! I'm so excited on the ride home, I don't fall back asleep. That and I'm worried about my baby. It'll only be a couple hours since we left her so she's probably still sleeping, but sometimes I wonder what Big Joe might do to her if left alone with her.

7

Sam

I'm running through the woods, still naked, holding Emma tight to my chest. I don't know which direction I should run, which way is the safest or quickest to get to some semblance of society, but any amount of distance I can put between myself and that fucked up family would be fantastic. Barefoot, I feel every stick and bramble, every pinecone and acorn, stabbing and slicing into the bottoms of my feet, but I push through the pain just to create more distance between us and the house, which I can still see behind me. It's as if I just left, it's so close.

I keep running until I realize I'm in my neighborhood, and facing my home. I run up to the door and try to open it but it's locked. I pound on the door with my free hand while my other cradles Emma, but still Jared won't answer. His car is in the driveway, so he must be home. I remember there's a hide-a-key rock near the front door and fish the key out quickly.

Suddenly, I get the feeling that lunatic family is after me, that they're on my heels, though they can't be, they can't have come this far. I fumble the key and it falls, disappearing in mulch. It's too dark now. I'm about to set Emma down to get on all fours and search when the door opens and it's Jared. I shout his name with relief, ready to jump in his arms in an embrace. Instead, I'm cut off. He shouts at me, "Can't you see I'm busy?!" with a phone to his ear. He slams the door and locks it, including the deadbolt. When he slams the door, it knocks me backward and I drop Emma. Emma's drop seems to be in slow motion but

I still can't react fast enough to catch her. I can only watch as Emma lands on her head.

I wake to Emma scream-crying from the other room. I know this cry. It means that she's dirty and needs a change. I can't believe it, but I miss changing Emma. I used to complain to Jared when he wouldn't wake to do it in the middle of the night and it seemed to always be me taking on this responsibility, not to mention every other responsibility when it came to our daughter. But I actually enjoyed those intimate moments we had together. Emma would quiet and stare up at me with those big watery eyes, eyes full of wonder and love. I could see that when Emma looked up at me, she felt safe. That's why she calmed down so quickly. I would get a warm feeling in my chest, which would spread to the rest of my body, and my eyes would grow misty. My eyes are misty now, just thinking of this.

I almost laugh at the irony of my current situation. Before, I was bitching that I was losing sleep because I was the only one who would get up to take care of the baby. And now, there's someone else here taking care of Emma, and as far as I can tell, she isn't abusing Emma in any way. There are no marks that I could see at least.

Hearing Emma cry like this is tortuous. It's why, at home, I would always pop out of bed and run to Emma's aid as soon as her cries wake me. There were times I would nudge Jared, trying to get him to take a turn. There were maybe two or three times he actually got up and tried to console her, but then he would give up quickly and hand me Emma, or just put her back in the crib with her still crying. Other times, he'd say, "Just let her cry," and then fall back asleep. When I brought it up the next morning, he'd double-down and say that that's what babies need, to cry for a few minutes, maybe 15 minutes, and then they'd learn to self-soothe. He'd read it online, he said. It just seemed like an easy excuse for him to not want to help out. Also, how was Emma crying not torture for him as it was for me? He could just sleep through it like it was nothing! I'm making myself mad just thinking about his apathy.

Emma continues to cry. *Where is that lady?* I think. Krystal's her name. Knowing their names might come in handy later, or might not matter. So far, Krystal isn't typically this delayed in stopping Emma from crying. *What's taking her so long?* I look to the door, expecting to see Krystal enter carrying Emma any second, saying that she's hungry or won't shut up. But she doesn't. Emma cries louder. I can picture her. Her face would be dark red by now, edging on purple. Being tied to a bed while my baby cries for me in another room is worse torture than anything else this psychotic family could do to me. *Are they doing this on purpose? Are they letting Emma cry like this to torture me?*

Then I hear someone else. It's a male voice but it doesn't sound like the old man. I look toward the door, trying to focus on hearing who this stranger is. Do they know to bring Emma to me?

"Stop!" he yells. Then he bellows loudly, incoherently crying in a mock of Emma but in a deeper voice, like he's trying to cover her cries with his own. Next, there's loud banging, like someone knocking loudly on a door or wall, along with Emma and the man yelling at each other. The banging stops as does the man yelling, and only Emma can be heard, her cries unabated.

There is a moment when Emma stops crying, which I recognize as the eye of the storm. You would think she has calmed down, but really, she is just catching her breath and then she will take on the wailing once more, stronger than ever. I only experienced this once, when I was still trying to figure out how to mother this new baby that had come into my life, before I had learned what the different cries mean.

In the lull, I hear a door shut somewhere else in the house. Almost right after the door closes, Emma lets loose, screaming even louder than before. The man screams "No!" from wherever he's at. A door bangs open and the man stomps out, likely toward

Emma. Seconds later, there's a loud thump, abruptly ending Emma's cries, then a softer thump. The man's footsteps move away and the door slams. The house is quiet. I can only hear the crickets and frogs outside.

I do not want to picture what I think I heard. It can't have been that, it isn't possible. Nonetheless, I sob, even harder than before. There is no way out of this. I need someone to come save me, save us. I wonder if Jared has begun looking for me, for us. He must have. I wonder if he is close to finding me, finding us. I should be in St. Louis by now, and it must have worried him that I haven't been answering my phone. *But how would he find us?* I look toward the boarded-up window, trying to push myself to be hopeful. Hopeful that Emma is okay and I am mistaken with what I thought I heard, and that Jared is looking for me, for us, and will find us soon.

8

Jared

I walk over to the window to my bedroom and open the curtains to let some sunlight in. I'm naked, but this side of the house faces the woods, so I don't have to worry about nosy neighbors getting an eyeful. When I stretch, multiple joints in my arms, chest, and back pop, loosening up my joints and sending tingles throughout my body. I look back to the bed where Anna is lying. She is still asleep, the silk sheets draped loosely over her perfect ass. Her back is to me, so I can't marvel over her perfect C-cup breasts, but I can appreciate the curve of her spine, and the fact that I can see some of the ridges of her spine.

A few months into her pregnancy, Sam really started putting on the pounds. She didn't really try to stay slim, she wasn't exercising, and she seemed to eat whatever she wanted. I didn't understand this because obviously one of the reasons I married her was being physically attracted to her, finding her sexy. But then she gets pregnant and gives up! And the baby comes, and she didn't lose all that much weight. It's impossible to continue being attracted to her. I suppose it would be easier if she wasn't such a bitch about everything. She's always getting on my case about something, whether it's how long I spend at work, some irrelevant chore that I forgot to do, that I'm supposedly not doing enough with or for the baby, or that I'm not listening to her when she would just start talking out of nowhere and I'm expected to catch every damn word.

She probably thinks I will apologize or something for

having to work when she said she needed to visit her mom. It's not like her mom is dying or anything. The woman had a stroke and she's fine now. Plenty of people have strokes and go on with their lives. I have too much to do to drop everything just to drive with her to fucking Missouri. The funny thing is, I tried calling her to see how her mom is doing, to pretend like I care, but she didn't answer, and she didn't even call me back. Admittedly, the day Sam left, I didn't try to call because I had told her I was too busy with work, which was partly true. Mostly I wanted to use Sam's absence as an opportunity to fuck my assistant Anna as much as possible. I know, it seems like a cliché, but maybe there's a reason it's so common. Anna's hot as fuck.

We were already seeing each other on the low. I didn't want anyone at the office to even have a sniff of what was going on between us. They could lord it over us, maybe even try to blackmail us if they were skeezy about it, or accidentally let it slip if they were stupid enough. The latter is far more likely than the former, but either way, I want to take no chances. Neither I nor Anna have any desire to end our marriages. We just want to have some fun now and then. And fun it is.

I had promised myself I would never take Anna to my house should the opportunity arise, that I would never sully my marriage bed, but Sam is being a real bitch lately, more than usual, so she kind of deserves this. I sort of hope she will smell Anna's pussy on the sheets when she gets back, just a faint hint of another woman, not enough to confirm anything, but just enough to make her question things and feel less about herself. I have to do something to keep her in check. She's becoming far too controlling, between the baby and trying to control my time. It's becoming unbearable.

This is partly why I took Anna up on the lunch date during work, which started with lunch and drinks and ended up at a nearby motel. I haven't had so much fun with sex since I was in my twenties. It feels so wrong and dangerous. We both came at least three times each in the thirty minutes we spent in that hotel room. Then we had the room for the night, so we told our respective spouses that we had to pull an all-nighter at work. "No, I'm the only one here," I told Sam. I told her there's a couch in the break room I would sleep on if I got too tired to work or drive. I made myself sound as apologetic as possible, and it worked. Anna and I fucked twice, fell asleep, then woke up and fucked again. I found that I had energy and vigor that I didn't have with Sam even when we were dating early on. I fucked Anna on the hotel bed, against the hotel wall, and in the shower. We fucked like a starving kid from China would eat if presented with a Thanksgiving buffet. And the best part was that neither one of us felt an ounce of guilt about it. If Sam wasn't such a controlling bitch all the time, maybe I would feel guilty, and maybe if Anna's husband Mark wasn't a fat slob with no libido, she might feel guilty, too. But as it is, this release is necessary to maintain our sanity, and so why should we feel guilty?

I go downstairs to start the coffee maker, then head back up to bed. It's the weekend and Sam would be out of town with the baby for days, maybe a week if I'm lucky, so we have plenty of time to kill. Anna and I will likely take the next week off just so we can screw as much as we want. She could tell Mark she's going on a business trip or something.

I slide back in bed, pushing myself against Anna's round ass, feeling it press against my dick, and start kissing her neck. I feel my dick twitch with the excitement of what's to come. She moans and grinds her ass against my cock, then turns her head so that we can kiss. She pulls me on top of her and we start kissing feverishly. Every time with Anna is like the first time. I guide my cock into her warm, wet pussy and push into her. She moans again, dragging her claws against my back. I fuck her faster and faster, gently nibbling on her neck, then biting her lip. She grabs at me and pulls me closer, bucking her hips. As she cums hard, she screams loudly in my ear, which when combined with her pussy gripping my cock tighter, causes me to explode inside her. I push in deeply a few last times, allowing her pussy to milk the rest out of me, then I roll over on my back. *Let Sam stay mad at me*, I think, then chuckle to myself, wiping my cock off with the sheets.

9

Daniel

Didn't I tell you not to talk to strangers?

Yes, Mommy.

And what happens if you talk to strangers?

The bad guys will take me away and I'll never see you again.

That's right.

I have a pounding headache, which is nothing new. Out of habit, I reach for my Advil but can't move my arms. I'm seated with my arms bound behind my back, like I'm under arrest, but with something rougher, like rope, with something hard and ice cold between my torso and arms. It feels like a steel pipe running from the ground, likely all the way up to the ceiling, though I can't see it. I can't see anything. Wherever I am, it's in pitch-black darkness. Either that, or I've gone blind. My eyes *feel* open and I don't feel anything over my eyes, but still, I can only see black.

The floor or ground beneath my ass feels smooth and hard, probably concrete. I try moving my feet around to find they are not bound like my wrists, that I can move them freely. Moving them also tells me I'm barefoot and likely not wearing any pants. I don't feel my shirt either, so I rub my chin across my chest to verify that yes, I am in fact completely naked. Above me, I can hear wood creaking, like footsteps, and thumps as well. I must be in a basement or cellar beneath the main house where I can hear the people moving around.

"Hello?" I'm hoping someone will hear me, but the

amount of noise above never pauses or alters. No one can hear me. I'm stuck here by himself with no apparent way out.

I kick my feet back then push myself up, rubbing my back against the pipe. The pipe joints scrape against my back sharply, causing me to wince and clench my teeth. I'm standing though, so I can change positions if needed. I feel around the pipe to see if there are any bends or loose joints I can work with, and try pulling at the rope outward and twisting my wrists, but neither seem to loosen the binding. I lean against the pipe to see if it has any give and it does seem to bend a bit, but perhaps that's just my imagination.

Upstairs, I hear shouting, though I can't make out what's being said. Whoever it is, is arguing. I can only assume it's my captors. There were certainly multiple. There was the old man, and whoever had put the rag over my face, which must have been chloroform or some other similar sort of agent.

I remember how I got here, generally. There was the old man in the truck, and someone else with the rag, but how had they found me? Were they just cruising around the mountain byroads, looking for hitchhikers or vagrants to kidnap? That doesn't make any sense. That road was empty when we got off the freeway, and it was still empty when I went looking for help. Either it was a crazy coincidence or they must have known that there was someone to pick up. I go back to the pile of deer bones that we ran over. If they were truly put there by a person, then it was a trap set for an errant car, such as ours. How they watched the pile, I have no clue. As far as I know, security cameras require Internet, whether it be wired or Wi-Fi, and we couldn't even get a signal on Ben's cellphone.

Where is Ben anyway? If I'm right that the pile of bones was a trap, then my captors likely circled back to pick up Ben. If Ben is lucky, he would have been still up in the woods when they returned. It would have been difficult for Ben to have gotten lost as any direction that was a downward slope would probably take him back to the car. But maybe Ben had hung out at the top for a while after having gotten some sliver of connectivity. If the connection was spotty enough, it would have taken Ben a while to find a nearby tow truck company that was able to go out to them. That's really all I can hope for, that Ben is okay. If not, then we are both fucked.

Across the dark room, I hear a noise, which sounds like an animal. I hadn't realized that something else is down here with me. My first thought is that it's something that could hurt me, and I regret shouting and banging on the pipe, but whatever it is, it hasn't stirred. So, the animal must be sleeping. I hear the noise again and recognize it for what it is – a snore. I was right, the animal must be asleep. The deepness of the snore leads me to believe that it's something big, like a large dog, but without vision I can't tell. It doesn't smell like a dog down here, but it doesn't really smell like anything besides a damp basement. My best bet for now would be to stay quiet and not upset the sleeping animal.

If I could, I would go back to sleep, but my aching head prevents sleep. It isn't as bad as it could get, but without my painkillers, I can expect that soon. I look up. Whatever argument was happening upstairs has ended. I listen for more footsteps, expecting someone to come to me, though I don't know what to expect from them if they were to come. Instead, the house falls silent above. They must have gone to sleep. I wish I could do the same.

10

Krystal

We get home about an hour later. Grandaddy doesn't drive so fast this time since we're in no rush really, well not as big a rush as when we're trying to get to our bunny catch. I've tried tellin' him before that it don't make no sense havin' the traps so far away, that it's a big risk that we won't get our catch if we have to drive an hour to get there, but Grandaddy always has a reason for what he does. He says we gotta spread 'em out real good, otherwise the police would know where to start lookin' if they ever got wise to what we're doin'. He says you don't wanna have a tiny little circle 'round your house. I said we ain't gotta worry about that. Like I said before, the traps are so natural lookin' that won't nobody raise no questions about it. They would just think some animal done dragged a deer over the road and left it there to rot. We only put the traps on roads that most people don't go down, and we only go huntin' in the fall, so that way we can hide the bones in the leaves and it makes sense. Plus, we don't even grab the bunnies every time one of 'em falls in our traps. We usually just grab one or two cars' worth which ain't much. So, one or two people go missing in the woods per year, that ain't no big deal. Nobody will notice it. Plus, sometimes we push the car over the edge so it looks like they had them an accident, if anyone ever finds the car which I don't think they do. I said to Grandaddy, we been doing this for years now, as long as I can remember, and nobody been sniffin' around here thinkin' somethin' was wrong. "Listen, Krystal," he says, "We don't shit where we sleep." And that puts an end to it. I know not to bring it up again.

We get back to the house and everything's all quiet, which is a relief. I was real worried that my baby'd start crying and there wouldn't be no one there to take care of her. My baby, Jolene —yeah, I think I'll go with Jolene—is so helpless by herself. Well, now that we got our two cars worth of bunnies, we can ignore the rest of the traps 'til next year when we set everything back up again.

Me and Grandaddy check on the boy bunnies in the pickup's bed and they're both snoozin' which is perfect. We could always knock them back out, if need be, but things go so much smoother when they stay down the first time. Grandaddy tells me to keep an eye on the boys in the bed of his pickup while he goes on in and fetches Big Joe. After a few minutes, they come out and me and Big Joe carry each boy down to the basement, while Grandaddy supervises. We pull off their clothes then Grandaddy tics 'em up. Tearin' off their clothes makes things easier for later, choppin' 'em up and all. Plus, you never know when someone might have somethin' hidden in a secret pocket, like a knife or somethin' else sharp, so it's best that we just strip 'em down. We shut off the basement light then head back inside.

Before going to bed, I need to see Jolene, so I walk on over to her crib but I don't see her. I move the blanket over even though it's pretty thin so there ain't no way a baby could be hidin' underneath it. My heart drops. That girl bunny musta got out somehow and took my baby and ran off. I stomp off to the Bunny Room and open the door and turn on the light all in one quick movement. But she's still there and she's cryin'!

"What happened to my baby?" she says, all crybaby boo-hoo-hooin'. What does she think she means, *her* baby? She's gotta realize by now that ain't her baby no more but *mine*. And what does she mean 'what happened'? She musta heard somethin' which makes my heart *drop* even further than it already was down. I go runnin' back to the livin' room where we got Jolene's crib, not even botherin' to shut the Bunny Room door, and I don't even need to look around or go ask Big Joe what happened 'cause I see her right there against the wall! My poor lil' baby Jolene is crumpled up on the floor near the wall like somebody's ol' babydoll they don't want no more. I go running over to my baby and scoop her up to my breast. Her poor little head is all dented in and one of her eyeballs is popped out. It ain't danglin' or nothin' but just all bugged out, and it seems flatter than an eye should be. Her body is all cold and limp against me. It musta been that asshole Big Joe who done went and killed her. Ain't nobody else it coulda been! I knew we shouldn'ta left them alone, I just knew it! Still carryin' Jolene, I go stormin' off to Big Joe's room where he's just snorin' away like nothin' happened.

"Big Joe, you wake up, you sonuvabitch," I say to him, givin' him a good kick in the side of his big-ass head.

"Hey, what you do that for?" he says as if I ain't had no right to be kicking him in the head, like it might make him any dumber.

"Look at what you did, you big, dumb retard!" I take Jolene off my chest and wave her in his face. She just jiggles around like she's made outta rubber. "You done killt my baby! I ain't had her but a coupla days and you went off and killt her!"

"I didn't mean to do it, Miss Krystal," he says. He always calls me that even though I'm his sister. "The baby, it was just makin' an *awful* noise. It made my head hurt so bad! You gotta believe me, Miss Krystal. I would'n do nothin' to hurt your things. Not on purpose!" He has big fat tears rollin' down his red face.

"What do you mean, you didn't do it on purpose?" I'm screamin' at him, even though it scares him. "You slammed her up against the wall! Look at what you did to her head! Look at her eye poking out, you lummocks!"

"Can't you see I'm sorry?" He's cryin' and beggin'. "Please don't hurt me, I won't do it again, I promise!" Big Joe's all curled up in a ball like a baby. Cryin' like a baby, too. He's coverin' his head with his arm, afraid I might hit him. I should do more than hit him, but Grandaddy wouldn't like that. And speak of the Devil…

"What the hell's goin' on in here?" Grandaddy comes in behind me, and he's already back in just his tighty-whities.

"Look at what he did, Grandaddy!" I say, waving Jolene in his face like I did with Big Joe earlier. He looks down at the baby but his face don't change none. He didn't care one wit about the baby, just knows that I wanted one, so us gettin' one would shut me up about wantin' a baby.

He turns to Big Joe and says, "And did you say you were sorry?"

"I did! Honest! I told Miss Krystal I was sorry and didn't mean to do it! That baby just kept cryin' and wouldn't let me sleep! I done asked it nicely to be quiet too, at first…"

"Alright, then," says Grandaddy, then he turns to me. "He says he's sorry. I don't know what else you expect to get from him. Now let's go to bed. It's been a long night and I'm tired. You should put that baby in the fridge, though. That's good eatin'!"

"But, Grandaddy…" I was crying now.

"Don't worry, sweetheart, I'm sure we'll get you another baby soon enough. We'll just tell Big Joe not to do it again, or he'll be on punishment."

There was no use in fightin' it. When Grandaddy says what we're gonna do, or lays a matter to rest, there ain't much you can say or do after. His word is law and we gotta respect it. I ain't happy about it, but I do as Grandaddy says and put Jolene in the fridge. I guess I shouldn't think of her as Jolene no more, just the baby, 'cause she's dead now. Maybe Grandaddy is right. Maybe we'll get a new baby and then I won't let this one out of my sight.

I oughta kill Big Joe for this!

11

Sam

My anxiety won't let me sleep after that. The house is far too quiet, something has to have happened to Emma. My ears are perked, waiting for any sound that would indicate that Emma is okay, but for what feels like hours, all I can hear is the muffled sounds of snoring. After hours of waiting, I hear the truck pull up to the house. So, they were gone, after all, the old man and Krystal. Where they had gone off to in the middle of the night, I have no clue. I hear the truck cut off and someone comes in the house. Soon, the snoring stops and there's two sets of footsteps heading out. They are outside for a while. Then there's another door, somewhere in another part of the house and what sounds like the people going heavily down a flight of stairs, then the sounds fade away. I start to wonder if they have left again when I hear a door open and the people moving around again. It sounds like at least three people, maybe more.

The woman, Krystal, comes into my room abruptly. I try to ask her if she knows anything about what happened to Emma, and she only screams at me, then leaves again, leaving the door open. Then I hear Krystal wail. I can then hear a conversation between Krystal and a man she calls "Big Joe." He must be the one who stayed home while the other two (three?) went out. I hear them say what happened to Emma, and my soul is carved out from my body. I don't cry, I may have run out of tears. My chest is heavy and my throat feels thick. I stare off at the ceiling, letting my vision be burnt by the overhead light. I lost my own light, my reason to be. I am nothing without Emma. Now I just wish the family would come and kill me and end this immediately.

The next morning, the old man comes in. I stare blackly at him as he passes the threshold. "Looks like Krystal left the door open last night, and the light on. She don't pay the 'lectric bill, I'll have to talk to her about that," he says more to himself than me. He starts disrobing, removing the straps of his overalls and pushing them down.

"Where's my baby?" I say through my teeth. I know Emma is dead but I still want to hold her body one last time, to feel her weight against me.

"I'm your baby now, bitch," the old man says and climbs into bed. I expect him to try to rape me, so I squeeze my thighs together as best I can with my ankles tied to separate corners of the bed. But instead, he huddles up against my belly and begins sucking on my breast again, this time my right breast. He smirks while he looks up at me, his wrinkled lips pursed, wrapped around my areola. His lips jut out almost comically like a duck's bill. I feel my milk let down, my body betraying me, and the old man responds with an exaggerated "Mmm, mmm!" as though mimicking the Campbell's soup commercials, without letting go.

On my belly, I can feel his penis growing hard. He grabs at my left breast and squeezes, causing milk to squirt out across his back. "Mmm," he hums and begins humping my belly, while continuing to suckle my breast. A mixture of the old man's drool and my milk drips thickly out of the corner of his mouth and down the side of my breast. He squeezes my left breast again, squirting milk on my face. He presses again, this time squeezing his hand from under my breast in an obvious effort to point my nipple toward himself. My breastmilk cascades down his back. He continues to hump me in twitchy, jerking movements.

The old man bites down on my right nipple with his sticky gums, then pulls while biting down, until my nipple suction-pops out of his mouth. He puts it back in his mouth again, sucking even harder. Painfully hard. He continues squeezing my left breast in rhythm with his humping, squirting milk everywhere. Both of our bodies must be soaked with it. Finally, I can't take it anymore and I draw my knee up as far as it will go, which isn't far, and as hard as I can, I push it up. My knee connects with the old man's scrotum, causing him to say "Oof!" and shakily curl up even more deeply, the ridges of his spine jutting out of his back like a dinosaur's spikes. He rolls off me and falls off the bed with a thump. He lays on the floor for a full minute, long enough for me to wonder if he's unconscious, or I killed him, before pushing himself up again. "You ought not'a done that," he says. I can tell from the large wet spot on his underwear that kneeing him in the balls made him ejaculate in his underwear. He leaves the room with a huff.

I'm left once again on my own, this time covered in my own breastmilk, the smell a terrible reminder of Emma. My heart aches anew, but still, I do not cry.

The old man comes back with something in his hand and a fat wad of tobacco in his lower lip. I don't look at him, but just continue staring at the ceiling. He bends over and clicks something into place, which I can't help but observe. He's plugging in a clothes iron. He sets the iron on the table while it heats up, then leaves the room and comes back with a large knife, and sits down. I don't know what the iron is for, but I welcome death, so I'm not afraid of the knife. I hope my death is quick and painless, but even if it's not, at least there will be an end to my misery. I go back to staring at the ceiling.

"I know you don't like it when I play around with your titties," the old man begins. "You made that pretty clear just now." He spits tobacco juice onto the floor. "At least not yet. But you might get to likin' it. In fact, I hope you do. But you know you can't be hittin' me like that or I can make things so much worse for you." He waves his hand in front of the metal side of the iron, then quickly taps it. It's still cold enough for him to touch. "You should know those are *my* titties now, not yours, and when I'm thirsty or hungry or horny or bored, I can suck on 'em whenever

I want." He stares at me, fixedly, waiting for me to challenge this command, and when I don't, he continues. "So, what you need now is to be taught a lesson. Let the forfeit be nominated for an equal pound of your fair flesh!" I assume he's quoting something biblical and don't care enough to ask. Regardless, he is insane.

He waves his hand in front of the iron again and seems to be pleased with its heat because he gets up from the chair. "Now I *would* ask which titty makes the most milk, but we already know the answer to that, now, don't we?" He gives my left breast a firm squeeze and it again betrays me by jettisoning milk across his arm and onto my belly where there is already a puddle of cooling milk. "So, we'll let that one be."

When the meaning of these words sinks in, my half lidded eyes pop open. The old man grabs my right breast and lifts it toward my chin. A bit of milk leaks out but it doesn't shoot out like my left breast. In his other hand he holds the large kitchen knife, which he brings down onto my right breast, starting at the armpit and slicing down. A sharp line of pain blazes across my chest and I immediately begin fighting against the restraints, arching my back and pushing away from him as much as I can. All I can do is writhe against the restraints, though. I can do nothing to stop him, but only delay his progress.

I had thought I had become numb, but the old man proves me wrong. The pain is worse than the time I had sliced my finger open while cutting lemons and got lemon juice in the cut. If I move my chest up, his arms move with me. He works the blade in slow, careful, sawing motions. The pain is like fire blazing from my chest throughout my body. My body screams and so do I. The old man says calmly, "Just a pound of flesh, no more and no less."

I see the blade slip out on the other side and nick my left breast, though I can't feel this happen. It still feels as if the blade is cutting through my right breast. I squint my eyes, fresh tears welling. Warm blood soaks down my body, mixing with the chilled milk, and to the mattress beneath. I begin feeling dizzy, and when I look down and see that in place of my right breast is a puddle of deep red blood, and that the old man is now holding what looks like a fatty cut of meat, and that the cut of meat has a nipple protruding from it, the world goes white.

I wake to my chest feeling a renewed sense of being on fire. There's a sizzle, bringing my attention back to my chest. The old man has the hot iron to my chest, mashing it down. Steaming, boiling blood comes rolling out the side, smelling like something between cooking sausage and a handful of pennies. I push my back into the mattress as if I can get away from the iron. The old man lifts the iron and surveys his work, then presses it back down about an inch away from where he had it, causing another sizzle and another jolt of fiery pain to rocket through my body. The iron is unplugged but very hot. He still holds my severed breast in his left hand while he stops the bleeding with a hot iron in his right. He smiles at the completion of his task, then walks back over to the table to retrieve his knife.

"I bet there's still milk in this sucker," he says to himself and pops the bloody nipple of the severed breast in his mouth, then suckles. Bright red blood covers his lips, but sure enough, he's able to get milk to come out, creating an orange mixture which foams around his grinning, toothless mouth. Blood drips down between his grasping fingers to the floor. He keeps sucking on it as he walks out of the room, leaving the door open and light on.

I shudder with the pain singing throughout my body, blossoming from where my right breast once was. I still don't dare to look at my burned flesh. I can't look, not yet, so I look to the boarded-up window and try to listen for the outdoor noises but hear none. My screams probably scared all of the wildlife away. Instead, I hear the old man come back to shut and lock the door. I also hear that, while doing so, he is still sucking loudly on my severed breast.

I breathe deeply, hoping to ease the flaring pain that throbs at my chest and emanates throughout my body. The room smells like my cooked flesh, which is nauseating. I'll never eat fried pork again. Despite this, my stomach grumbles. I haven't been given food or water since I arrived with Emma. It's been at least two days and I am dehydrated and half-starved.

They clearly don't intend to outright kill me, which would be a blessing in that it would end the pain of having lost Emma, and now the physical pain constantly throbbing loudly. The old man said that this torture he just inflicted was meant to serve as a lesson. I am meant to just take it when he comes in to use my body as he wishes. If I fight back, it only ends in more pain, more torture, but not death. I don't think he would remove my other breast, as then he wouldn't be able to feed from me, but there are plenty of other body parts to remove if he sees fit, and plenty of other ways to torture me, far exceeding my own imagination, which doesn't require the permanent removal of pieces of my body.

The only way out of this is to escape or die trying. With my hands bound, I can't even kill myself if I wanted. Either through death or escape, I'm determined to find a way out. I look up at the ropes binding my wrists, staring hard at them as if I can will them to unravel themselves. Even when I first got here and my strength was fresh, I couldn't do anything to budge the knots or to break the ropes. Plus, my arms ache from being held up for two days. I'm losing feeling in my hands.

I look down to the ropes around my ankles, which seem just as sturdy and tightly knotted, if not sturdier. But my legs are stronger than my arms, and they are pinned down instead of held up. If I'm going to be able to pull any of my limbs from my bindings, it would be my legs. But say I am able to get my legs out, what then? I'm not flexible or strong enough to lift my legs up to my wrists and untie my hands. I'd still be stuck here, and on top of things, I'd end up pissing off the old man even more and he'd hurt me again. As I bounce between considering escape and giving up, I doze off, my mind seeking a respite from the pain.

12

Krystal

From my bedroom I can smell Grandaddy cookin' meat, a bit surprising since I thought we'd be cuttin' into our bunnies as a family. That's what we normally do. Turns out he'd done went and cut off one of the girl bunny's titties and was fixin' himself breakfast. It does smell good, though, so I help him serve it up. There ain't much meat in a titty, it's mostly fat but damn if it don't taste good! Somethin' about the milk glands inside soakin' in through the fat of the titty meat makes it super tender and melt in your mouth delicious!

Even though I'm mad at Big Joe for him killin' my baby, I have to cut him a slice too. I have to keep the peace. Big Joe's still sleeping so his plate sits with his meat gettin' cold while me and Grandaddy eat. Grandaddy really enjoys his titty meat, him havin' the biggest piece on his plate. His eyes roll back with every bite. I can hear the click and pop of his dentures grindin' the meat into a mash before he slurps it down. He don't want no drink to go with breakfast, don't want nothin' to mess with the flavor of the titty meat, but I like coffee in the mornin'.

While he was still cooking, I started a pot of water boilin', so I could have a cup of coffee with my meal. Other than the slurpin' and smackin' we're quiet until we both are all done eatin'. I guess the girl bunny had done somethin' to piss him off so as to make him cut her titty off.

"I was thinkin' we'd cook up one of the boys in the basement for lunch," I say, hopin' to take his mind off my baby in the fridge.

"Don't want that good baby meat to go bad," he says and gets up from the table.

"I... I don't think I can eat her, she was my baby you know." This is goin' to lead to my idea, but I have to take it careful 'cause I want him to say yes. "So, I was thinkin', Grandaddy," I say trying to sound like his sweet, little girl again. I stop to make sure he's payin' attention. "Seein' as you said I could have a baby and we done waited two years after you said that I could before we even found us a baby... then dumb ol' Big Joe done went and killt Jol— I mean, that baby... I was thinkin', I was thinkin' maybe I could *make* me a baby." I swallow. I'm nervous he's gonna say no and then it would be done. "I could fuck them boys in the basement before we kill 'em, you know? And once I'm lit with baby, *then* we could kill 'em." Grandaddy seems to be considerin' it so I keep talkin' so he can't say no just yet. "I'd take care of the baby, just as good as I took care of the last one. *And* I'd just birth the baby in the bathtub like Momma had me, so we wouldn't need no doctor. And we'd have us a baby who'd grow up into a kid and a teenager and a grownup who could be helpin' us catch more bunnies."

"I don't know, Krystal, it'd just be another mouth to feed."

"Maybe after a year or so when she's done drinkin' my milk, but you ain't had a hard time huntin' deer, and then there's the bunnies. We got a freezer full of meat in the back room!"

Grandaddy thinks about it for a minute then says, "Alright, Krystal. I suppose it's fine. But that baby will be *yours* to take care of, and if you die birthin' that baby it'll be your own damn fault."

"Thank you, Grandaddy!" I kiss him on the cheek. "I promise, I'll take care of the baby! She'll be *my* responsibility."

About that time, Big Joe wakes up and comes outta his room. I don't want to start in on him again so I run off. I'm nervous about how this'd go. This would be the first time I done fucked a real man. No, I ain't no virgin. Up until I was fourteen, Grandaddy had me goin' to school with the rest of the kids in town. The school bus would come pick me up from about a mile down the road which I had to walk in the mornin' and afternoon every day. I don't know why Grandaddy wanted me to go to school. I guess to make us seem normal, not that anyone needed to care one wit what happens in our house or who we have here. Maybe it was to learn how the world outside is. Big Joe ain't never had to go school because he's retarded.

So, I went to school all the way up until I was fixin' to go to the ninth grade, which is high school, when they started askin' for a social security number for me which I ain't got one of them. Grandaddy says I ain't got one because I weren't born in a hospital, I was born in a bathtub. Anyway, while I was goin' to that junior high school, they had a dance called homecomin' and I went to it because this cute boy asked me to go with him. He even had his daddy pick me up from the end of the road and I wore one of Momma's old pretty dresses. After about three songs he took me under the bleachers of the gym, pulled my panties down and put his pecker in me even though I didn't want it. I didn't mind, not really. I figured that's just what boys do. It hurt a lot as you'd expect but I got over that. Plus, I was on my period so he couldn't get me pregnant. That boy, John was his name, went and told all his friends that I let him fuck me, so they wanted to fuck me too, and I had to let them because I didn't know no better. One time they all fucked me, takin' turns on me in the bathroom durin' P.E. class. So, between the social security number thing and Grandaddy findin' out that the boys been fuckin' me, he said I was done with schoolin' and that was that! Like I said, what Grandaddy says is what goes.

Since then, I been stuck at home except when me and Grandaddy go to set up or take down our traps, when we pick up the bunnies, or when we go to the grocery store for all the stuff we eat besides meat. When he goes huntin' for deer, he takes Big Joe along, not me. He says he needs me to mind the house since he's gone for a week or two every time, and Big Joe only gets to go because he can carry a deer for miles.

So, yeah, I get the itch like any woman would but I ain't never fucked one of the bunny boys before. Grandaddy says it's best I didn't. Instead, I just go back in the field behind our house which used to be a cornfield and still is though nobody tends to it anymore. Grandaddy says that when he was a boy, he used to help his Daddy mind the field, but even then, it was gettin' overgrown with weeds and they couldn't keep up with it. They ain't had no money to be hirin' help, so it was just them. Since then, Grandaddy and me and Big Joe have just let it go to shit. There's still corn in there which we'll go through and harvest by hand if we want some to eat, but otherwise the field just sits there gatherin' weeds and snakes.

I got the idea once to get me a corncob and use it as a fuckstick and I been doin' that ever since. It's only fair anyway. Grandaddy and Big Joe can jerk off as much as they want, so why can't I? I'll get the itch and will sneak off to the cornfield 'cause I don't need Grandaddy or Big Joe knowin' my business. I don't need to go too far to be hidden, nor to find me a nice hard corncob. I'll shuck it first so I'm not puttin' the strings in my pussy, plus the little corn bumps feel pretty damn good. I'll plop my bare ass on the dirt and fuck myself with the corncob until I shake with my cummin'. I'll picture somebody from TV like one of them strong bare-chested men from my soaps. In my head, ol' Billy Abbott or Adam Newman or Dylan McAvoy will be there plowing me in the field with his big bumpy corn cock. I'll let myself moan out figurin' Big Joe and Grandaddy can't hear me from the house. Then when I'm done, I'll throw the corn to the ground and it didn't take long before I got a good pile goin' of all my used-up corns. I thought they didn't know about what I do out there in the cornfield, especially since I only do it once a week or so when I get the itch, but one time, I caught Big Joe in the cornfield sittin' on the ground next to my pile, gnawin' on a corncob, smilin' and droolin'. He looked at me like he knew what I been doin' and he laughs his big stupid laugh, little bits of corn all over his big round face and beard. I swear, that Big Joe, I could ring his neck sometimes.

So yeah, I ain't no virgin, but it's been years since I had a real dick, and this will be the first time that I'd be doin' the fuckin' instead of gettin' fucked, so I'm nervous. Course I want to get started before Grandaddy changes his mind or before I change mine. I go on into the basement and turn on the light. I don't know which one I wanna fuck to be honest, so I suppose I'll pick one when I get there. Just thinkin' about this is gettin' me all slick!

I get down there and believe it or not but the white one, the one who turned out to be a soldier 'cause of what we found in his wallet, is still asleep! He ain't dead neither 'cause he's snorin' as loud as a bear! The other one, the black bunny boy, is awake, or at least I wake him up when I turn the light on. He's all squintin' because his eyes ain't used to the light yet. They're both naked as I said before, so I can size 'em up, though I figure the choice has been made for me 'cause I ain't sure if the sleeping boy's cock will work unless he wakes up.

So, I turn to the black boy and smile. He asks me why we took 'em here, which I usually don't answer when the bunnies ask that same old boring, dumb question, but this time I'm feelin' generous and in a good mood so I go and tell him. "You just happened to be at the right place at the right time. You're just lucky, I guess," I say to him.

That answer don't seem to make him happy, but I don't care. I go over to him and he starts to scramble back, probably thinkin' I'm fixin' to hurt him. That'll come later I suppose but for now he should like what I'm fixin' to do. Before he can get too far from me, I grab onto his cock, which stops him dead in his track. "Don't you worry about it, bunny," I say to him.

I pop his soft cock in my mouth tryin' to get it hard for me to fuck. His cock tastes good, like eatin' bunny food raw almost. It's salty from his sweat I guess, is nice and hot, and a bit musky. I can feel his cock gettin' harder in my mouth while I suck him but I keep goin' 'til it's as hard as I can get it. He's breathin' all heavy and gettin' into it. He's probably wonderin' why I'm doin' this but he ain't complainin'. His cock is gettin' real big and thick but it ain't all the way hard yet, not as hard as I've seen dicks get in pornos.

Compared to those boys who fucked me back in school and the corncobs, this bunny boy's cock is real big, so big I start gettin' worried it won't fit in me. But I make it work. I sit on his cock and let it slowly slide in my pussy. I can feel it stretchin' my pussy out which hurts, but in a good way. I push up and down slowly a couple more times so my pussy juices go down his cock and grease him up. Once my pussy gets used to his size, I can start fuckin' him faster. I just bounce up and down on his dick, listenin' to him moan beneath me. I can't believe I'm fuckin' me a real man! Before I know it, I'm fixin' to cum, so I start fuckin' him faster and harder. When I cum, it feels like a rush of electric tingles runnin' through my whole body. My pussy grips him harder making his cock feel even bigger, makin' me feel a second cum comin'. He's huffin' and moanin' but he won't cum yet, so I pull up my t-shirt and let my titties out to give him somethin' to look at.

13

Daniel

I'm bewildered by being woken up abruptly with blinding light. The first thing I see is that what I took to be an animal in the room with me is actually Ben, still asleep and snoring. Before I know it, a half-naked petite young woman with a mop of unkempt dirty-blonde hair and a greasy face struts in, then instead of giving me answers or doing anything I expect really, she starts sucking me off. *This might explain why I'm naked*, I think.

I'm left speechless by this dirty woman sucking my dick until I get hard. She's admittedly attractive for a dirty hillbilly, which is what I take her to be, but I suppose any woman would look hot while giving head. "Trailer-park treasures" my coworkers at Applebee's would call women like this. Soon, she's bouncing on my dick, fucking me fast. Her pussy feels warm, wet, and tight, almost virginal, but I'm too woozy from whatever drugs they gave me to really enjoy this. Plus, I'm getting raped, which dawns on me partway through. I didn't realize men could be raped, not by women anyway.

I feel her orgasm as her pussy grips me. She slows with a shiver, then keeps going. She pulls her shirt up so that her small tits bounce in my face. She even leans down so that her perky nipples drag across my cheeks while she rides me. The girl starts breathing heavy in my ear, then nibbles on my lobe, which when combined with all the sensations causes me to feel an orgasm building.

Right as I'm about to go, I see that standing next to me

is an old man—it dawns on me later that it's the same old man who picked me up from the roadside the night before. The old man is wearing nothing but a pair of briefs pushed down to his ankles. He's jerking off his uncircumcised dick toward us. If I wasn't so close to ejaculating already, I would have lost my erection, but instead, I shoot inside the blonde girl as she rocks her hips back and forth, grinding her pussy against the base of my dick. Feeling me explode inside her apparently causes her to cum again. I can feel her pussy grip me harder than before and she shakes with the second orgasm. All of this must excite the old man because then he cums, spraying semen all over my chest. I can feel the warm spatter as it lands and I'm immediately revulsed. I even feel a drop or two hit the side of my face.

The girl hadn't noticed the old man until then because after he sprays me, she turns toward him and says, "Grandaddy, what the fuck?!" This just makes the old man chuckle with a wheeze and trot away while pulling his underwear back up, leaving us with a look at his sagging ass as he makes his way up the wooden stairs. The old man's spunk lazily drips down my ribs, onto the basement's concrete floor. The girl huffs, then slides carefully off of me. She stands above me, my own spunk dribbling out of her vagina and onto me. "Ah, damn it!" she says, and starts hurriedly scooping it up with her fingers, then dabbing them into herself. Watching this, my eyes get heavy. The sex has caused my migraine to dissipate and a post-coital warmth is spreading over me, making me drowsy. I let sleep take me.

When I wake sometime later, the girl is gone and I'm cold. I can feel my migraine starting to creep back, and I can feel the stickiness of the old man's dried semen on my chest and belly, and worst of all, face. The best I can do to remove the sticky spot is rub my cheek on my shoulder.

"You awake?" Ben asks from across the room. He too is bound but to a large metal ring in the wall. It's probably half an inch thick and rusted over. He's seated against the wall with his hands bound above him. Like me, he's naked.

"Yeah, I'm awake." I continue to rub my cheek against my shoulder.

"What are you doing?"

"You don't want to know." I try to get a good look at the ring binding Ben but it's about fifteen feet away and my vision is blurred. Fortunately, the distance also makes it so Ben likely won't be able to see the dried semen on me and the floor next to me, saving me from having to explain what happened just moments ago. "Have you tried pulling at your restraints?"

Ben looks up, then says, "Yeah, but I can't give it much effort. I'm fucking tired, bro. Somebody drugged me, I think."

Ya think? "Yeah, I think that's exactly what happened. To both of us. These people are fucking crazy. We need to get out of here before they kill us. Or worse." I almost laugh at the irony of the situation. Prior to the road trip, I was seconds away from killing myself. And had the road trip gone according to plan, I probably still would have once we got back home. Maybe found a hotel or something. "Do you remember anything about how you got here?" I ask. Ben shakes his head. I fill him in on everything I remember up until waking up here, in what is essentially a dungeon. I tell him that as far as I'm tracking there is an old man and a younger woman, but there may be more of them. I don't mention that the woman fucked me against my will, though I did enjoy it until the old man decided he wanted to join in the party. Then I remember something. "Last night I heard an argument. I couldn't tell who it was but I don't think the old man was one of the people shouting. So, there's got to be three, maybe four people keeping us here."

"Why do you think they kidnapped us?"

"I have no clue," I lie. My initial assumption was that we were kidnapped for the purpose of torturing and murdering, the kind of stuff you see in movies. I'd also watched enough serial killer documentaries to have an idea of how many crazies there are in this country. But then, what happened with the girl, or more specifically, what happened at the end when she was scooping up my semen and pushing it back in herself, indicates there may be something other, or at least something more. She seemed pissed when my semen fell out of her and she seemed all too eager to get in back in there. She's trying to get pregnant. What doesn't make sense to me, though, is that she isn't hideous —in fact, some would say that she is on the hot side of the scale —so why does she feel the need to capture men to rape them so that she can get pregnant? I'm sure she wouldn't have trouble finding a willing participant should she hang around the local bar or high school football game.

Upstairs, I can hear people moving around. One set of footsteps definitely sounds louder than the rest. It could be someone stomping, or it could be someone very, very large.

"So, uh, what's the plan?" Ben says.

"Well, besides getting out of these ropes?"

"Yeah, what are we supposed to do? Just sneak out past who knows how many people are up there? Then, what? Go running around outside naked, with no clue where we are or where we need to go? Considering where we were picked up, we're probably in the middle of nowhere. So, what are we supposed to do?" Ben is short-tempered again, something I chalk up to his PTSD.

"I don't fucking know, alright?" Sure, there's his aggression, but still I don't know why Ben expects me to have all the answers. I can't even keep my own life together, and that was before cancer decided to go ahead and cut my life short. I suppose that's why I started playing my little game, if you could call it that, with the revolver and the whiskey. I don't like the idea of cancer, or anyone else, being the one to tell me when I can or should die. If given the choice, I should be the one to take my life.

14

Krystal

"Grandaddy, what'd you do that for?" He don't give me no answer, just goes on whistlin' and grinnin'. He's cleanin' the dishes from breakfast.

He asks, "Do you know why I told ya before not to be screw our catches?"

I'm a bit confused by him changin' subjects. "No, I figured it was another one of those 'don't shit where you eat' lessons."

He laughs and coughs, shaking his head. "No, Krystal, but that would serve here as well." He sets the dishes he's holdin' in the sink and turns around, then pulls his wrinkled cock out. "Take a look at my pecker." He holds it in place, lettin' me get a closer look. It's quite a sight, covered with bumps and pus-filled blisters, all angry lookin'. He's got extra skin hanging down over the head of his dick which he pulls back to show that the head of his dick is wrinkled and gray but the opening is rimmed red as a crabapple. All the times I done caught him jerkin' off I ain't never actually looked at his dick, and can you blame me? Who'd want to look at their Grandaddy's cock? Now I know why he was always itchin' it or pullin' at it through his overalls.

"Got all these bumps from puttin' my pecker in one of them bitches," he says, wavin' his hand in the direction of the Bunny Room. "I'm just sayin' is be careful is all. You done picked the one you fancy—and hell I can't blame ya, I like some dark meat from time to time myself!" He breaks up in another round of cacklin' and coughin'. He pounds himself on the chest then pushes his dick back into his briefs. "So, you might wanna to keep it to just the one, that's what they used to say on TV anyway. I say yer better off in the cornfield than fuckin one of those boys." I feel my cheeks get warm and I'm sure my eyes pop outta my head. "Oh, don't go blushin' on my account, I ain't never seen ya go out there, I only heard about it from Big Joe. He musta seen ya go out there some night. I don't mind one lick! Hell, it might even make the corn grow better!" He set off laughin' again. "Anyway, I only said it was okay for you to fuck 'em because you wanted a lil' baby so bad and it's about time we added to the family anyway. If you don't want me to interrupt your lovin', I'll keep to my own." Grandaddy tilts his head and gives a puppy dog look.

"No, it's alright, Grandaddy, you just surprised me is all. If you wanna watch me fuck them boys, that's okay, I don't mind."

"That's my babydoll." He comes over and gives me a kiss on the forehead. "I was about to start fixin' lunch. I know you didn't want none of that babymeat so I can cook you up a venison sammich."

"That'd be great, Grandaddy, thank you!" I'm over the moon happy! I start to get up when he says, "Can you fetch that bitch some water? It's been a coupla days, don't want her dyin' on us. Not yet anyway."

So, I do as Grandaddy asks and fill up a glass from the faucet. I give him a kiss on the cheek for his kindness then run off to give the girl bunny her water. When I get in there, her face is all red and she looks like she's been crying but she also looks pissed. She still has the one titty, so Grandaddy did do her that kindness lettin' her keep a titty. Where the other one was, now is just a big ol' nasty burn lookin' like Freddy Krueger. There's blood all over her tummy and some on the floor, probably from when Grandaddy cut her titty off. There's also a little blood on the table in the shape of the knife he used.

"Brought you some water," I say holdin' up the cup. She

looks, but don't say nothin'. Her face is asking if I done poisoned it, but why would I poison her water? If I wanted to kill her, I'd just do it. I wouldn't pussyfoot with poison, I'd use a hammer or a knife or my own two hands. So, I sit down and let her watch me smoke a cigarette and sip on her water. "Guess you probably know by now the baby is dead." The bunny sniffles but don't say nothin', just looks at me all pissed like she can intimidate me. I could laugh!

"What did you do to Emma?"

"Her name was Jolene, and I ain't done nothin'. My stupid brother killt her." Then she just screams at me, which I gotta admit makes me jump.

"Fine, bitch, if you don't want water, you can just sit there and stay thirsty." I drop my cigarette in the glass of water and it sizzles out. I get to the door then think of somethin' real funny. "I'm just gonna leave this door open for ya." She looks over all confused. "That smell you're about to smell? That's the baby, fryin' up like bacon. And if you listen real good you might even hear her little head pop when it hits the pan!" And I leave her there screamin' and cryin' like Jolene used to do.

I didn't like doin' that joke because it feels like I'm bein' mean to myself, too. Jolene was my baby just like the baby was hers before she brought her for me. *It's alright*, I tell myself. *I'll have a new baby soon, and best of all she'll look just like me!* Though Jolene did look like me, she didn't look like my twin like my new baby will. I can't wait to get pregnant! I'll have to try again after lunch!

I come back to the kitchen and Grandaddy's so sweet, he's making my venison sandwich first! I don't mind it cold, but he heats it up with cheese on the frying pan. As soon as the meat hits the frying pan and starts to sizzle, I hear the girl bunny screamin' all loud again. *Whoops!*

"Did you not shut the door?" Grandaddy says turnin' the venison over in the pan. He peels the plastic off the Kraft slices and puts them in there with the deer meat.

"She was bein' a bitch to me, dint even want her water," I say.

"What'd you say to her?" Grandaddy says, turnin' away from the pan.

"Nothin'," I lie. "She just thinks we're tryna poison her I bet."

"Sounds like she needs another lesson already." Grandaddy shakes his head, then slides the cheesy venison on some toast on a paper plate and hands it to me.

"I can try again, maybe starin' at that water made her rethink her decision." I walk back to the room with my sandwich and sit back in the chair by the water. "You thirsty yet?"

"Fuck you," she says and she looks mad as a hornet. I ain't got nowhere to be so I take a bite out of my sandwich, meat and cheese fallin' out the bottom on my lap and she just turns her head and throws up a mess of yellow bile. No warning, she just pukes on the side of the bed! She puts her head back down and her hair goes in her own upchuck, but she don't seem to notice. She's just cryin' and makin' the nastiest face.

"You're lucky I got an iron stomach," I say and take another bite. Then I come to realize that she done threw up because she thought I was eatin' my baby! I can see why she would think that 'cause I just finished sayin' Grandaddy was gonna be cookin' up the baby and then I walk in with a steamin' hot meat sandwich. I guess I forget sometimes not everyone knows the difference in smell and look between deer meat and people meat. I take another bite and lick my lips.

15

Sam

Krystal is seated across from me again, seeming to gloat. When she walked in and sat down the first time today, I couldn't help but notice that her panties were soaked, which was disgusting but not as repulsive as her suggestion that they would be dining on my child. The blonde laughs and tells me that the meat she's eating is just venison. I've always been the expressive type and my face must make my confusion apparent. Krystal explains that it's deer meat. I can still taste the acidic bile on my tongue and can't push the thought of this maniac eating my child like a hamburger out from my mind, causing me to dry heave.

"Listen, do you want the water or not?"

Still grimacing, I nod emphatically, and she brings the water over, leaving the plated sandwich on the table. I'm very thirsty, so much that my throat burns. I'm surprised that I can still produce tears considering that my captors haven't yet given me water, or food for that matter, since they brought me in at least two days ago... or was it three? My weariness is playing with my mind and I'm losing track of time.

I open my mouth, allowing Krystal to pour the drink. When the cool water touches my lips, I can't help but feel blissful and close my eyes. Gulp after careful gulp, I take down the water, which tastes very minerally. This would make sense if it's well water as is likely the case, and it smells like... an ashtray. I had forgotten Krystal put out her cigarette in the water earlier. I make this realization too late as the cigarette butt slides down my throat. I can feel the small mass bump along my esophagus, far too along for me to stop its progress. I cough and splutter, and Krystal takes the glass away.

"Alright, don't choke now," she says. "I don't wanna have to do CPR on ya, I ain't no dyke. Though I'm sure Grandaddy would be happy to oblige." I shake my head just as emphatically as I had nodded for the water and Krystal laughs and says, "Suit yourself." She leaves the room with the half-empty glass of water, locking the door behind her.

I can still smell the meaty aroma from the sandwich across the room, which thankfully has supplanted the smell of my own cooked flesh. Krystal had called him "Grandaddy." I can't help but look at the plated sandwich and feel my mouth start to water, another interesting event considering my dehydration. My stomach grumbles loudly as if to say, "Okay, you've had some water, now feed me!"

The notion that the sandwich is not deer meat as the woman claimed, but in fact my poor Emma-Bear, fileted and cooked like a holiday ham, brings on a competing feeling of nausea. I'm stuck between the immense sick feeling and starvation when Krystal reenters the room to retrieve her forgotten sandwich. She takes another giant bite of the meal as she walks by causing me to regurgitate again, this time all of the water I just drank, as well as some bile, onto my burned chest. It stings anew, though the pain had never really left. Krystal leaves the room, shaking her head as if I had intentionally thrown up all the water she just gave me.

I look down at my chest with a wince. It looks bad. Really bad. There are areas where the cut hasn't been burned which are scabbed over and inflamed. The burned area is worse. My flesh is inflamed and dark red. It takes me a moment to realize that it isn't skin I'm seeing but exposed muscle, fat, and sinew. There wouldn't be skin; he'd chopped off my entire breast, then used a hot iron to close the wound in the most painful way imaginable.

The image of the old man walking around sucking on my severed breast reenters my mind and I shake my head vigorously to free myself of this vision. I've already thrown up more than I care to for one day, so it makes no sense to think of disgusting stuff like that.

I let my eyes wander, up and away from my missing breast, when I catch something that seems impossible. My right thumb has somehow slipped out of the rope binding my wrist. I don't know when this happened, though it was likely when I threw up, one of the times anyway. Feeling a sense of renewed energy, I pinch the four fingers of my right hand and manage to slip them out of the rope entirely.

I immediately twist over to untie my left wrist, but have trouble pulling at the knot. In fact, I have trouble with manual dexterity in general as my hands have been bound for days now. My fingers move sluggishly and I have difficulty gripping the rope. I likely made this knot worse on my first day here when I pulled at the knot as if the ropes would magically unravel and ended up tightening the rope. I pull my left hand closer, as far as its length of rope will allow, in the hope that the decreased distance will allow my right hand extra strength from not needing to reach as much. I manage to get my index finger's nail into the knot and excitedly pull downward. Instead of the knot coming looser, my fingernail is pulled halfway off my finger.

I shove the finger in my mouth both to stifle the need to scream in pain and to apply some pressure to the wound. While I continue to work the knot, I use my remaining fingers while holding my index out to prevent further damage. I manage to get a solid grip on the outer bump of the knot between my thumb and middle finger, this time using the pads of my fingers instead of my nails. I push them together as hard as I can manage to maintain the grip, trying my best to ignore my screaming index finger. Blood is leaking down my hand. The knot loosens maybe a millimeter. Using the same two fingers, I find another part of the knot to loosen it and grip it just as hard, then pull as hard as I can. Instead of loosening the knot, my fingers slip off of it, leaving mild burns on both finger pads—very mild compared to the burning sensation in my chest. I try again at the same knot part and am able to get it to move though almost imperceptibly. I go back to the part of the knot I had moved first to see if I can loosen it more when the door opens and the old man walks in with a paper plate of mashed food.

"Aw, what the hell," he says, dropping the plate to the floor with a splat, and runs to grab my free arm. I swing at him wildly, only grazing his temple with my fist. He moves out of the way before my hit can connect. Even though he seems old and frail, he's fast and strong. He easily overpowers my free arm, pulls it back to the rope, and reties the knot. He does this with little effort, not even bothering to call for help.

He checks the knot on my left arm to ensure it's still tied. "Now, how the hell did you do that?" He doesn't seem angry, just genuinely curious. When I don't answer, he says, "Well, I was gonna be nice and give you somethin' to eat but seein' as you're trying to be a regular ol' Harry Houdini, we'll have to make sure you can't get out no more."

The old man leaves the room and comes back several minutes later with the iron again, but instead of the large knife he had last time, this time he brings a pair of garden shears. "The good news is you won't need those ropes on your wrists when I'm done." He plugs in the iron and sits down. "I guess you just got lucky somehow and were able to slip the rope. You do have such dainty lil' hands, it's no wonder."

He notices my fingernail and walks over. "Oh, my my, what happened here? That looks like it hurts a bitch, don't it?" He pops my index finger in his mouth and sucks on it, then withdraws enough to run his tongue between the nail and exposed finger. "I don't know how many girlies I've had here in this bed, but I think you might just taste the sweetest."

He returns to his seat. "I had your titty for breakfast and

my-oh-my that was the sweetest cut of meat I ever did taste! It just melted in my mouth! I almost was tempted to cut you a slice just so you could see for yourself, but I suppose that woulda been a waste since you prob'ly woulda just spit it out."

As the iron heats, it starts to smoke, further cooking the burnt blood left on there since this morning. For a long moment, the old man just sits and stares at me, expressionless. I stare back in an effort to fight against what I perceive to be an intimidation tactic. The old man interrupts the silence. "Do you know what they used to do in the old days with thieves?" I know the answer but don't dignify him with a response. "They'd chop off their hands. Do you know why?" Again, I don't respond. "It's to remove the part that causes *offense*. That way, the thief can't steal no more. Makes sense, don't it?"

Instead of waving his hand in front of the heating element part of the iron, he places it face down so that more steam emits from the sides as it burns the lacquer or enamel on the small table. "So, I come in to feed you, and I see you whittlin' your little fingers away at the knots, and what do you think is the appropriate punishment for that?" I know where this is heading and begin to sob. "I was hoping not to have to punish you again so soon, you know? I mean you lost a *lot* of blood last time, and there's more food to be had than from little ol' you. But maybe this will learn ya."

The old man unplugs the iron and brings it over to the right side of the bed. This time, he plugs it back in and sets it on the floor. He goes back to the table and retrieves the gardening shears. "Now you gonna make this easy for me?" I don't want to make anything easier for the old man, so I ball my right hand into a fist, which pushes my index finger's nail back further. I can hear it rip. The pain is immediate and makes me get lightheaded. "Now don't do that. I can just break them first if you want." I trust that he will keep his word and shakingly open my hand, fingers splayed, hand trembling.

He puts the blades around my pinky finger and lops it off with one quick movement. Blessingly, I faint. But, as before when the old man had severed my breast, I wake to the searing pain of him stemming the bleeding with the hot iron.

"Please stop," I beg. "I won't try to get out again, I promise. I'll be good, I'll do whatever you want." This last sentence causes him to hesitate, but he doesn't stop and readies the shears.

"I'd like to trust you," he says, "but you haven't done anything to earn my trust." With a quick chop, my right ring finger is also removed from my hand and falls to the floor. I don't faint this time, but black stars circle my vision. He carefully sets down the shears, picks up the iron, and burns the new wound, the blood hissing. I know that if he wanted to, he could easily chop off more than one finger at a time, maybe even all at once, but he clearly is taking his time, relishing the moment.

As if confirming this, his erection is once again visible through his stained briefs. I crazily think, *he clearly doesn't need Viagra to help him in that area*, and begin laughing out loud, feeling maniacal. "You mind lettin' me in on whatever's got your goose?"

"You should do commercials," I laugh through the pain, tears welling. "Instead of paying for the little blue pill, men could just could get hard from torturing women! You'd make millions!"

"I don't get it," he says then chops off my middle finger. The room swims. Each time he chops off a finger, a jet of bright red blood shoots out of the new wound like a water gun. The flesh and blood cooking under the iron smells like sausages. I can no longer feel the pain in my hand so much, my mind saving me from much of the torture to come. He chops off my index finger with its broken nail and I almost laughingly thank him. That nail was a real bitch after all.

Just when I think he's done, he readies the garden shears one last time, poised over my thumb. My hand is completely coated in blood, with black scorches where each of my fingers once were. By the time he's lopping off my thumb, he's broken out in a sweat and his erection is nearly pushing out of the flap in the front of his underwear. I'm thankful that it stays put. Lastly, he uses the shears to cut the rope, letting my right arm fall to my side. Only then does it begin to throb with pain.

"I'll get your left hand tonight. Let you grow some more blood," he says. "Then you'll have both wrists free and you can clap your hands for your dinner from now on! You can be like a circus seal!" He gathers up my digits from the floor, then carries them out of the room along with the iron and shears. I'm still between laughing and crying when he comes back to turn off the light, shut the door, and lock it. My right hand thrums with pain, taking my mind off the pain on my chest. I'm not sure which hurt more, but the hand is more recent and currently wins the most painful event in my life contest, if there ever was one, beating out giving birth to Emma even. Remembering Emma, I sober and begin crying in earnest. I no longer want to escape. I have no desire to see Jared or my family again. Without Emma, I have nothing. I wish the old man or the blonde would just come in here and slash my throat. Maybe if I'm lucky, I'll die of blood loss.

I stare at the boarded-up window again. Normally, windows, with their views outside, represent freedom. The painted wood running across this window gives it the opposite impression. The room aptly speaks of restriction, it shouts control.

16

Daniel

Our conversation is cut short by the door opening. The blonde enters the room and shuts the door behind her. "Hey," she says to me. "Ready for round two?"

Instead of acknowledging her question, I ask, "Why have you taken us here?"

"Ugh, you always ask the same question," she whines. "You bunnies are all the same. Okay, sure, I'll play this time. Do you want the truth, or an answer that'll make you feel better?"

"The truth," Ben says sternly, as if he can really intimidate someone while tied up naked to a wall.

"Oh, look who's awake. Welcome to the land of the living! The living dead! Ha!" She smirks at him. "So, you want the truth, eh? It ain't gonna change anything, and you're gonna find out soon anyway, so I guess I might as well tell ya." She looks Ben dead in the eye. "You're food. You're bunnies we catch in the woods, who we string up to keep the meat nice and fresh for as long as we can while we take off little pieces of you to keep our bellies full."

"You're lying," I say, wishfully.

"'Fraid not. We might keep *you* around a bit longer, at least until you've served your other purpose..." She looks pointedly at my crotch. "But then you'll be food, too. And I bet you'll be delicious. I gotta say, I will miss that cock though, but not too much. It hurts a little to be honest."

"What is she talking about?" Ben asks.

"You're welcome to watch, soldier boy," she says with a big toothy grin. In response to Ben's shock, she says, "Oh, we know. We checked your wallet and found your military ID. You look real stupid in it, by the way. Oh sorry." She quickly stands at attention and slaps the back of her left hand to her forehead in a mock salute. "Sir, yes, sir!" The blonde giggles then turns back to me. "Alright, enough questions. Let's get busy."

Before I can protest, she again has my cock in her mouth. It's soft so she's able to fit the whole thing in her mouth which she sucks on hard without moving her head. With her right hand, she grabs my balls and squeezes, a little too roughly, causing me to wince. When she releases me from her mouth, I've grown only a little and am not erect.

She pretends to pout. "Oh, c'mon, why won't you get hard for me?" I start thinking of whatever I can to keep from getting hard – baseball, the fact that I have cancer, that old man jerking off on me. "Do you need to see my tits again?" My cock involuntarily twitches. "Yeah, I bet that'll do it." She lifts her shirt again, revealing her small, perky breasts. Her pink nipples are already stiff with excitement. She brushes one against my lips, making my cock harden a bit more.

I hold a slight amount of power in that she's clearly trying to get pregnant, so if I can prevent that for as long or as much as possible, then I may be able to stay alive for longer. I also realize that I'm fighting a losing battle. She puts me back in her mouth and starts sucking me off faster and faster. The blonde pulls a rubber band out of her constant-bedhead hair and wraps it around the base of my cock, twists it and wraps it twice more, creating a makeshift cock ring. She pushes her panties aside, slides on me and begins rocking her hips with her hands pressed down on my chest, fingernails digging into my flesh. Her tits are still free from her shirt and bouncing in my face, her hips moving feverishly now. I don't fight it anymore and let myself release inside her. She slows down and then stops, but doesn't get up. It takes me a moment to realize that she's trying to keep my semen inside her for as long as possible.

"Hey, can I go next?" Ben asks, and the girl whips her head around in frustration. The phrase seems to be triggering to her.

"No, you're too ugly," she says, then looks down at Ben's crotch. "But your cock is pretty. Looks so good, I could eat it up!" She turns back to me. "No offense, sweety, your cock is real pretty, too. And real big, unlike your boyfriend's little pecker over there." She slowly slides off of me. I can feel her squeezing on it, but realize it's not for pleasure. She's trying to keep my sperm in her as she lifts off of me. Her face looks pleased, indicating that she believes she's succeeded. She moves the crotch of her panties back over with her thumb then walks over to Ben. "Let me a get a closer look at that pretty cock."

Ben's dick is already hard from watching her fuck me. He no longer seems to be worried about being held captive, not being as perturbed as I am about the situation. I look away, not wanting to watch my best friend have sex. "Aw, fuck yeah! Let's fucking gooooo!" Ben shouts, and I wish the old man would come down and give Ben a taste of what I went through. "Bro, I think we should stay here a long time!" Ben shouts across to me.

Has Ben already forgotten about what the blonde said about us being food, or does he still think she was kidding? Though I'm looking away, I can't help but hear the wet slurping sound of the blonde sucking on Ben's dick. This ends abruptly with Ben screaming. "What the fuck?" I look over and Ben is flailing his legs wildly, his body twisting, while the girl stays connected to his crotch. Ben pulls back a leg and kicks the girl in the belly, knocking her backward.

"Who the *fuck* do you think you are?" The girl screams and gets onto her feet. She makes a run at Ben and kicks him in the crotch, shutting him up immediately. Ben's face turns purple and his head jerks to the right. He starts gagging like he's going to throw up. The woman goes around to the other side of Ben and punches him in the face, then storms out of the room.

Once she's gone, I ask, "Are you okay, man?"

Ben splutters then looks over, pissed, as if it were me that wronged him. "She bit my fucking dick!" I stifle a laugh. Perhaps it's schadenfreude, or more likely it's how much of an asshole Ben has been this whole trip and how he didn't seem interested in trying to get out.

"Well, she *did* say we're food, that the plan is to eat us."

"Shit, bro, I'm bleeding! My dick is fucking bleeding!"

I can't help but look, as one does with a car crash. Ben's dick does look red, but it's certainly not bleeding profusely like he's making it seem. "Do you still want to stay here for a long time?"

"Fuck you, bro. How come all she does is suck you and fuck you, and when she gets to me, she bites my dick?"

"Listen, it doesn't matter. We need to get the fuck out of here. She might be fucking us, or me, now, but I think she was being serious that she and the old man are going to eat us. We're dinner."

"Bro, I don't think your dick is looking too hot either." I look down and notice that the woman left the rubber band on me and my dick is still hard, and purple. With my hands bound, I can only use my thighs to try to remove the rubber band, but I can't get an appropriate grip on the band. "You look real fucking stupid doing that," Ben says, smirking. I stop trying to remove the rubber band and give Ben a look as if to say "fuck you," then huff and look away.

After a long, painful hour of waiting, the woman returns, with the old man in tow. He's wearing his denim bib overalls again. The old man is carrying a large dirty toolbox. The two make a beeline for Ben. "What's this I hear about you kickin' my Krystal in the belly?"

The blonde—I now know her name is Krystal—pipes in, "I could be pregnant already and you coulda killt the baby!"

"You know what they did in the old days?" The old man sets the toolbox near Ben. "If you was a thief, they'd chop off your hands. If you were caught lookin' at another man's wife, they'd take outcher eyes. And well, son, your legs have been causin' trouble from what I hear."

"You ain't doing shit, old man!" Ben draws his legs up to his body as though ready to deliver another kick.

The old man laughs as if hearing a joke that he's heard many times before but that doesn't stop being funny. "C'mon, Big Joe, what's keepin' ya, boy?" he shouts in the direction of the door.

"Sorry, Grandaddy!" booms a deep voice. We all look toward the doorway and see a hulking man with a beard. He fills the doorframe as he enters. As he gets closer, I can see that one side of his head is dented.

"Grab his feet, boy," the old man commands and the large man dutifully obeys. He grabs Ben's ankles and pulls his legs straight. No matter how much Ben struggles, he can't compete with the large man's indomitable strength. The old man calmly opens the toolbox and withdraws a heavy black belt, a small handsaw and a red metal canister with a nozzle which I initially take to be a fire extinguisher.

"What the fuck are you doing?" screams Ben, panicking. He's able to wriggle his body in an effort to pull away, but his legs remain glued to the spot in the floor where the large man holds him. It seems Ben is more likely to pull the ring out of the wall and free his hands than he would be to break out of Big Joe's grip.

The old man slips the belt under and around Ben's left leg, loops it, and tightens it with a hard pull. Soon I realize it's a tourniquet. With the tourniquet secured, the old man pulls out the saw which was clearly made for removing errant tree limbs, not body parts, and begins sawing at Ben's leg beneath the knee. Ben's face, which was so recently dark red, edging on purple, loses all color. Blood rushes out of the fresh wound but it's thick, dark, and slow-moving, the tourniquet stopping any excessive blood loss. The sound of the saw going through Ben's shin bone —the tibia, I strangely recall from my high school biology class— causes me to vomit. Ben appears to be in shock.

When the saw breaks through to the other side, Ben's thigh jerks upward, no longer held down by the rest of his leg, by the large man. I can see the bottom of Ben's knee cap—*his patella* —as well as a severed chunk of his tibia in the midst of the meat of his leg, which is still steadily seeping blood.

The old man, calm as ever, grabs the red canister and strikes it to create a flame, then blows fire onto Ben's bleeding stump. I can smell cooking flesh, as well as Ben's leg hair being singed. Ben passes out and remains passed out while the old man begins working on his other leg. His face is pale and I start to believe he's dead when he jerks awake, again screaming. "Boy, you scared the shit outta me!" The old man stops sawing to shake his head, spits tobacco off to the side, then resumes his work. Big Joe is still pinning both of Ben's ankles to the floor, even though one of them has been severed from his body. The old man repeats the procedure on Ben's right leg then returns his tools to the box.

"You don't have to hold his feet down no more," Krystal says, rolling her eyes, arms crossed.

Big Joe looks blankly toward the old man for guidance. "She's right, go on and take them feet upstairs to the fridge." Again, the big man dutifully complies, though he pauses to look at me as he passes, confused. I recognize the look. I experienced it many times on the road trip, and many more times before. It's the look of someone who's never seen a black man before.

As the remaining pair are about to head upstairs, the old man says offhandedly, "You might wanna take that rubber band off his dick. It looks like it's fixin' to fall off. Unless that's yer intent!" The old man guffaws, leaves the room, and the blonde scrambles over and rolls the rubber band off my dick, which has half-softened but couldn't go all the way down with the rubber band on it. Krystal has a face like she is considering fucking me again but reconsiders and leaves, bringing the rubber band with her, rolling it back into her hair.

I look over to Ben, whose skin is pale and who is hyperventilating, staring at his leg stumps which he has lifted off the floor for closer inspection. A large pool of blood leads from his legs to the center of the room, slowly moving toward me.

"Hey man, I know this sucks but you need to calm down," I say. Ben just keeps breathing fast, then he stops breathing altogether. He stares wide-eyed at me and starts convulsing. I scream for help even though I know they intend to kill us anyway, only hoping that they will help Ben so that we can live just a bit longer. I don't want Ben to die in front of me, not like this. I continue to scream until I grow hoarse. I was already dehydrated before I was kidnapped, hungover from the night before, and the people keeping me captive haven't brought me water or food.

I didn't cry when I got the cancer diagnosis, nor did I cry in church when my mom and the pastor had everyone pray for me and they cried. Staring at my childhood best friend, watching as the convulsions cease and Ben collapses, eyes remaining open and fixed on me, I cry. What begins as a sob quickly turns into a big ugly cry, tears streaming down my face. My headache comes back with a vengeance, but I ignore it as best as I can.

"Ben," I say. "Are you okay, man?" Ben is motionless and unblinking. "Ben, wake up, man." I know Ben isn't sleeping, but keep trying to wake him anyway. "Hey, man, I think we can get out of here. We just need to slip out the ropes. No problem, right?" Ben continues to stare, as if waiting for more information, as if waiting for me to elaborate on the plan. I can no longer stand it and look away from him, staring into the corner of the basement. When I squint, heavy tears fall down my cheeks.

There, in the corner, are several stacks of boxes. I have trouble reading most of them through my bleary eyes, but can read one. It reads, "Corn Star® Pure Lye! Drain Opener".

17

Sam

Distantly, I think I can hear a man scream in pain. It sounds like it's coming from far away, maybe outside, perhaps on the other side of a mountain. The room is swaying as though I'm on a boat, rocking at sea. I ignore that this is from blood loss, dehydration, and starvation, a terrible mix for one's health. I pretend it's just the gentle lapping of waves against a cruise ship.

I think back to when Jared took me on a cruise, one of those big ships that are on the cheaper end to get on but are still fun. Through a free room upgrade, plus some help from my parents, we had a balcony suite. Jared spent a great deal of the cruise imbibing, going to the bar for hours without me, drinking and "just making friends," he said. I trusted him—I *trust* him I mean—but it was a bit disheartening getting the feeling that I was spending much of the vacation by myself, and so early in our marriage. I made the best of it, lounging by the pool with a book, and sure, I would have a few drinks each day as well.

Toward the end of the cruise, when I brought my concern to Jared's attention—it was important, many friends and family members told us, to communicate with your partner —he immediately went on the defensive, saying that he was just trying to have fun. And besides, he said, I was giving him the impression that I wanted some alone time. "Am I supposed to just sit there while you're reading your romance books by the pool and not do anything?" I was so affronted by this I couldn't respond. I wasn't used to being in a relationship that was so—rarely, but *still*—tenuous. Jared wasn't like this before we were married, but within months of our union, he became a different person. He wouldn't say why, nor even acknowledge that anything had changed.

I did find peace on that cruise, being at sea for the first time, even though I was essentially alone. I would hang out in the stateroom, hoping to catch Jared when he came back, but then find myself sitting on the balcony, my book resting at my side, temporarily forgotten while I got lost in watching the hypnotic waves undulating and lapping against one another. Tiny silver fish jumped out from the boat's wake hovering for dozens of feet while black and white seabirds dove to catch them. I still smoked then, and though it was against the cruise line's rules, I smoked from the balcony, tapping my ash into a glass which I would rinse in the sink when I was done, after flushing the cigarette butt.

This small detail from my memory brings me back to the here and now, as the connection of the cigarette butt rolling down the cruise ship's stateroom toilet brings to mind the cigarette butt that recently washed down my throat with the glass of water. While I know it's impossible, I can feel it in there. It's a lump in my stomach, stewing, releasing its poisonous carcinogens. The room has settled, mostly. My crotch starts to burn, which takes me too long to realize that I'm urinating, soiling myself once again. *Great, a UTI to go along with everything else.*

The house again becomes relatively quiet. The birdsong outside informs me that it's still daytime. Since the light was left on and my vision is blurred, it's difficult to discern through the gaps in the boarded window a general time of day. I fantasize about a small bird flitting on the windowpane, unseen, and carrying my message, my cry for help. I imagine it flying through the forest and somehow reaching my mother to tell her that I'm in trouble.

My mouth twists down as I realize that it's highly unlikely

that Jared is looking for me, at least not yet. We weren't on the best of terms when I left to see my mother, so he probably assumes I'm intentionally ignoring his calls. *Is he even trying to call?* I wonder where my phone is, if these freaks kept it or got rid of it. It's a pointless idea to consider, since it's a longshot anyway for me to get out of this room, much less find my phone elsewhere in this house, if it's even here.

Now that I've been mutilated and tortured in other ways, I come to the conclusion that my time here is fleeting. I know now that waiting for someone to come and save me is not really viable. The odds of someone finding me before it's too late are smaller than my songbird delusion actually happening. I must escape, but not be caught doing it. If I'm caught again, I'll lose more body parts, making it all the more difficult to escape.

My first step is obvious – get my left hand free. With my left hand available, I'll be able to untie my ankles, which is step two. I look to the door, the one obvious escape from the room. I consider the locks I've heard click into place, but also the fact that the old man and Krystal have both at times neglected to lock the door. They know the door only to be secondary, that it would be about impossible for me to get off the bed. The door is just your standard wooden interior door from the looks of it, so I believe I would be able to knock it down if given the opportunity, though that would be noisy and draw those people's attention.

And that's the other part, I'll have to do this in the middle of the night, while everyone's asleep. Now that my Emma-Bear is gone, there will be no reason for them to wake up in the middle of the night. I don't know the layout of the house, but know that with enough time and if I'm careful enough, I'll be able to figure my way outside. I consider the fact that I'm naked and don't have a phone, which means that I will have to venture outside without clothes and with no way to communicate with the outside world. If I'm quiet enough, I may be able to look around for some clothes and my cellphone, or *a* cellphone at least.

I look to the window, my Plan B. If the door is locked and the people are still home, it would be better to try to pry the boards off the window, then climb out. I would have no opportunity to gain clothes or a phone, but I would be out and have a chance to run as far as I can and hide somewhere at the very least. It's a terrifying thought, but it would be worse to stay here.

I am again discouraged. If the old man does to my left hand what he did to my right tonight, I would never be able to escape. Unless, that is, I can give him a reason to let me keep my hand. I know what I must do.

A few hours later, more or less—time is impossible to accurately gauge in this room—the old man reenters with a new plate of food. This time, he carries a sandwich very similar to what the girl had before, as well as another glass of water which looks a little murky but potable at least. "You ready to eat this time?" he asks, as though I weren't ready to eat last time.

"Yes, sir," I say, and the old man seems momentarily taken aback by my politeness.

"I see you learnt to be good already, and it only took two punishments. Or one and a half." He shakes his head, chuckling at his own joke. "Better than some, worse than others. What do you want first?"

"The water, please."

He sets the plated sandwich on the bed next to me, then puts the glass to my lips and tilts it slowly, tenderly. I look at him the entire time I drink and he smiles at me, almost lovingly. My throat is scratchy and it actually hurts to swallow, but I force my way through it and am able to do it without wincing. After I down the entire glass, I sigh, a tingling sensation emitting from my core, my body thanking me for finally drinking some water. "Did you just have a cum?" the old man asks warmly.

I again stifle a grimace, this time from the old man's

repulsiveness, and instead smile and nod at him. "I think I might have. I needed that water, I'm so thirsty."

The old man bites his lip. "I can get you some more in a little bit, but I don't wanna give you too much too quick. You'd get sick up all over your titties... or titty I mean."

"You can suck it if you want. It's full of milk right now, just for you," I say in a purr.

"Don't tempt me!" The old man grins, his mouth full of yellowed teeth. *They must be fake,* I think. *He was toothless earlier.* "Anyway, you need yer supper. I don't want you losin' *too* much weight." He grabs my thigh with a squeeze, taking me back to the truck where this hell started. "Now, eat slowly, I don't need you chokin' on me."

"I thought men liked it when women choked on them." I feel gross flirting with him but have to keep up the act if I want to keep my hand.

"Ooo wee!" The old man slaps his thigh and nearly knocks the sandwich to the floor. "You are quite the slut-whore when yer hungry aintcha?" The old man scoops up the sandwich with both of his gnarled hands and presents it to me. The meat smells succulent and greasy, somewhere between a cheesesteak and a barbecue sandwich. I open my mouth with my tongue out, just as Jared liked me to do, just like the porn stars he liked to watch. "You keep openin' yer mouth like that and I might hafta put my pecker in there," the old man says, placing the corner of the sandwich in my mouth.

"You can do that too, if you want." I say before taking a bite, making eye contact with the old man to give him a sense of sincerity. The very notion of doing anything sexual with this revolting excuse of a human makes me want to vomit, but I know that if he desires me, he may want to keep me around a while, and not be inclined to continue "punishing" me.

The juiciness of the meat bursts in my mouth, making my

mouth water more than it already was. My stomach grumbles in anticipation of the hot food making its way down. The old man is in his overalls, but he grabs his crotch in a way that indicates he's getting hard. His face shows his horniness too as he feeds me another bite, which I take willingly, making sure my lips wrap around the sandwich sensually. I can hate myself for this later, but for now, I must play the role.

"I can't take it no more," the old man says and begins disrobing, his denim overalls slipping to his ankles. As I guessed, his dick is hard, pushing against his yellowed briefs. I begin to wonder if he's been wearing the same briefs day after day or if he has many pairs with similar staining. He pushes his briefs down, freeing his dick, which much to my chagrin, is worse than I expected. The first thing I notice is that he's uncircumcised, which isn't the most unsettling aspect of his genitalia. It's covered in pustules, bumps, and scabs. The old man pulls the infected looking foreskin back to reveal the gray tip of his penis. There appears to be black mold spots all along its surface and his urethral opening is a deep red, a stark contrast from the gray tones of the rest of his head. Surrounding the base of the head is a thick white film of skin and oil. A tiny drop of fluid rests at the opening of his urethra, either pre-cum or urine.

He sidles up to the side of the bed, pressing one boney knee on the edge of the mattress. He presents his cock to me, expecting me to take him in my mouth. And wanting to stay alive and relatively whole, I oblige.

I close my eyes, hoping to give the impression of sensuality but in reality, attempting to ignore the vileness of the act. When the head of the old man's dick enters my mouth, I'm met with the taste of sour milk mixed with a taste comparable to how mildew smells. The folds of his foreskin rub along my tongue and catch on my teeth. He withdraws and thrusts back in deeper and I can feel the bump of his sores rubbing along the roof of my mouth. To prevent myself from vomiting, I tell myself that I'm simply mouthing a bumpy vegetable, something amorphous like a gourd. Inside my mouth, one of his bumps bursts, splashing my tongue with a salty brine. Again, the old man withdraws slowly and thrusts back into my mouth harder. I vaguely notice that he has one hand on my remaining breast, squeezing the milk out. On my tongue, I feel the crumbly mash of oil and dead skin extract from his cock—it's called smegma, I randomly remember. The rubbing action from his dick head paints my tongue with the grit and oily paste which has a fishy taste to it. My mouth salivates with the strong aromas and flavors, albeit repugnant. I allow my slobber to fall from my lips, not wanting to ingest a single drop of this vile concoction. He pulls nearly free from my mouth, allowing my lips to drag along the length of him, then pushes forward with great force, knocking against my teeth and forcing my mouth open. My teeth scrape along his shaft as he pushes in, bursting another one of his bumps. The thought crosses my mind to bite his dick, try to bite it off if I can, but I know this will only make my situation worse. He thrusts as deep as he can go, his cock just reaching the back of my tongue, where it rests for a moment. The old man shudders, holding the back of my head so that my lips press against the matted thicket of his wiry gray pubic hair. I feel his dick pulsate and a warm fluid bead onto the back of my tongue, oozing out of his cock thickly. He holds my head against him until he's done leaking thick cum down my throat. He pulls his shrinking dick from my mouth, a thick line of saliva mixed with his semen dotted with grains of smegma stretching like mozzarella from a cartoon pizza. I hold everything he oozed and emitted in my closed mouth, hoping he will leave soon so that I can spit it out and likely vomit.

"Well, what are you waiting for, bitch? Swallow it." He stands akimbo, waiting. His now flaccid dick is red from the scraping and exertion. I hesitate for just a moment before pushing myself to swallow it. I think of raw oysters. It feels like a hot lump in my throat, catching there, threatening to cause me to purge the scant food I've eaten. But I force a smile, open my mouth and stick out my tongue to show that I've done as he commanded. His smile is victorious. "That's a good girl," he says and pats my thigh. "If you can figure out how to use that mitt, the rest of the sandwich is yours to eat." He gives my vulva a rough squeeze, then leaves the room, again neglecting to lock the door.

I count ten footsteps after he leaves, then turn over the side of the bed furthest from the door and wretch until I'm able to force myself to vomit out all of his dick detritus, along with the glass of water and small amount of food I had before.

After several long moments of allowing my stomach to settle, I reach for the remainder of the sandwich with my right palm, which is no longer a hand. I intend to grab the sandwich, but can only pat at it. On top of this, everything I touch with this hand causes pain to shoot from what feels like my fingertips, up my arm. I feel hopeless. If I can't do so much as lift a sandwich and take a bite, how do I expect to be able to untie myself?

Despite the pain, I bang the side of my hand on the mattress. In my head, I make a fist. I try again, this time sliding my right palm under the plate until it's at what I estimate to be the center and I lift it, balancing as best I can. My nonexistent fingertips send alarms of pain echoing along the corridors of my arm, but I push through the pain and lift the plate toward my chest. My right pectoral muscle, once covered by a breast, but now exposed and burned, joins the chorus of pain. But I press on. It's not about getting the food in my belly so much as it's about proving to myself that I can do this simple task. Still balancing the plate precariously over my body, I lift the plate up to my chin. I lean my head to the sandwich and take a bite from above, also scraping the plate with my bottom teeth. I chew, grinning with renewed hope.

I look to the bedpost where my left wrist is bound. It's tight. If I had a hard time loosening it with fingers, there was no way I would make any progress with my paddle of a palm.

There has to be another way, I think, reassessing my situation. I reach my right palm over and press on the bedrail and it, being made of wood, seems to bend or perhaps separate from the rest of the frame. Even though the pain in my hand is screaming for me to stop, I press again, and harder, pushing the bedpost off its nails by a millimeter or two. Not much, but still progress. I try it a third time, this time also pushing in the same direction with my left wrist. The bedpost's top nails pop completely out, with a small bang, also causing the entire bed to shift. The bedpost is still connected to the frame at its base but it now swings loosely from its top. I am elated and almost don't hear the approaching footsteps. I quickly pull the post back into place and the nails slide quietly into their former holes.

The old man enters the door swiftly. He's still sweating from his recent activity. "What was that noise?"

I'm careful not to look at the bedpost, or make any gesture that indicates something happened with it. Instead, I look down at the plated sandwich on my chest. "I just about had it in my mouth," I say sulkily, fully aware of the double entendre. "Then I dropped it and I jumped with the pain of it hitting my chest." *A plausible story,* I think, while I wait to see if he's buying it.

"I didn't think you had it in you." He actually sounds impressed. He looks to my chest. "Your other titty's gettin' big again already." He licks his lips.

I make my best attempt at sounding casual. "Yeah, this one's always filling up fast. You could help me with it, you know. If you want."

"There you go again, tryin ta tempt me!" His eyes are bright. "I would if I could but I fear if I start suckin' on that titty, my dick will get hard again an' I don't have it in me to do anything else just yet. Maybe in the mornin' I can help ya out."

"That's alright." I sigh, truly in relief that I wouldn't have to put up with the old man suckling on my breast again, at least not for a while, but hoping that it's perceivably a sigh of regret

96

that he's not jumping all over me keeping up with the pretense of Stockholm syndrome. "I can just mash down on it with my free hand"—*mitt*—"and that should tide me over until the morning." I feign disappointment that he won't help me now.

"Well, that'll do." The old man scratches at his crotch roughly. He looks back at the sandwich. "Damn good, idn't it?"

"Yes." I nod. "My compliments to the chef!"

"Real tender, ain't it? My favorite. It's too bad we don't come by this sorta meat often. I tell ya, if I had to pick my last meal here on Earth, this would be it."

I smile appreciatively. "It might be the best barbecue I ever had."

"Oh, it ain't pork. Pork comes cheap." The old man snorts wetly and spits a volley of mucus and tobacco juice. "That meat's yer baby."

Though the light is still on the room, my vision darkens immensely. I can no longer play along with his playful banter. I fold into myself and the rest of the world becomes shut off. I don't see him leave, but he does, and he shuts off the light when he goes. I don't know whether or not he locks the door, because I don't hear it. I don't hear anything. The sandwich is still on my chest, and I can smell it, and feel its weight pinning my body to the mattress. I can't feel my wounds or anything else except the weight of the plate, and I can only smell the meat. My baby's *meat*. My Emma-Bear reduced to nothing but an evening meal, which I took bites out of, not realizing, not thinking. I wish I could vomit again; I wish I could do anything, but I cannot even move. The connection between what Emma was and what Emma is interweaves and intertwines within me.

Emma was a weight on my chest, my sleeping baby.

Emma is a weight on my chest, my dead child.

My dead child.

Emma was my sunshine, her bright smile lighting the room.

Emma is darkness, a void.

Emma was life.

Emma is dead.

I stare down at the sandwich, though I can no longer see anything in the lightless room, with my darkened vision. What I see is Emma, alive and well, resting on my chest after having nursed. Emma, milk-drunk. Emma, snoring. I brush my free palm against my baby, against the bread of the sandwich. Tears streaming down my face, I sing a lullaby as I hold the meaty sandwich to my ruined chest.

18

Daniel

I understand that I will die here, tied to a pipe in a place no one will find me. My flesh will feed this sadistic family, and my bones will be broken to chips, or melted with lye until they are brittle and shattered until they are indistinguishable as human remains. I am only waiting for the inevitable, which may come in moments, or days, or weeks, but soon. Part of me wonders if the bullet actually pierced my brain in that apartment so long ago, and I was successful in killing myself, and this, this is just the afterlife. There is no way to escape this hell, only waiting until it ends, when *they* choose for it to end. I will wait until they come to visit again, to use my body for one means or another. Maybe I will be lucky like Ben and they will make swift work of me so that the pain is short-lived. But for now, I get to endure my migraine.

A tremor possesses my body, shaking my ropes against the pipe involuntarily, causing the pipe to rattle against its mounting in the ceiling. Coincidentally, I was worried about having tremors during the trip because I knew it would be difficult to explain them to Ben without telling him about the tumor. *Now that Ben's dead, I can have as many of these as I want.*

Above me, a toilet flushes and the pipe I'm tied to rattles in its now-loosened bearings. I reach up the pipe just for something to grab onto, but then, my eyes widen, once again alert. I find a bolted joint in the pipe, a wide octagonal piece which should be able to be twisted. With my hands, I'm unable to make it budge. I can only strain at it, causing my palms to become raw and my arm muscles sore. I'll keep working at it, later. Eventually, hopefully, I'll get it to start moving. If it's anything like a nut on a screw or bolt, once you loosen it initially, it moves much more smoothly after that. For now, I feel weak and despondent. I guess that is to be expected when one witnesses their friend getting murdered for the simple act of kicking out when their genitalia is bitten.

The old man had asked the big man to carry the severed limbs to the fridge. Coupled with what the girl had said, I know they likely plan to eat the meat from Ben's legs as their evening meal. If she is to be believed, and I certainly believe, somehow Ben and I have stumbled upon a family of cannibals and we're on the menu. *Great, just great. What are the fucking odds?* I can't help but see the irony in our predicament. If the round meant for my dome had come a chamber revolution earlier, I would not have been alive to answer Ben's phone call to join him on the road trip. Ben may have still driven from Seattle to Chesterfield, but he would not have ended up here. From this, I realize that it's my fault that Ben is dead. If I hadn't made such a game of it and just offed myself like a man, Ben would probably be home right now, eating his mom's cooking. Instead, he's seated across from me, his eyes perpetually positioned on me, staring, or more appropriately, glaring.

After hours of waiting and hoping that the migraine, the tumor, would just do me the service of ending things, the door to the basement opens and in walks the girl again. I know why she's here but I'm in no mood for hanky-panky. I wasn't in much of a mood before, but she got me hard enough to jump my bones, and was able to make me cum inside her. She's going to keep doing this until she's pregnant and then she'll discard me, disposable as I am.

"I brought you some food and water," she says, almost meekly. I hope that it's poisoned. I take the water in great swallows, which causes my migraine to abate a bit. The food is some sort of ham sandwich on toast, which I eat greedily. It's moist and delicious, but I assumes its palatability is mostly due to how starved I am. Whatever it is, it's a very fatty meat, but tender, reminding me of veal or suckling pig. Her mind seems to be elsewhere as she holds the sandwich in front of my face so that I can eat.

"Thank you," I say. I know my captors have no plan to let me free, but I figure being polite might at least facilitate them being nicer.

"Whatever," she says, looking away. A single tear rests on her cheek.

I wonder if it's my place to ask and dare the possible intrusion. "Everything okay?" I try to convey concern.

She sniffles, glances at me, then back to the corner of the room. "Yeah, I just miss Jolene."

I take another large bite of the sandwich, barely chew it, and swallow the food. I'm worried she'll change her mind about feeding me and I want to get as much food on my stomach as possible. "She a friend of yours?"

The blonde sniffles again. "No, she was my daughter." Her hand holding the sandwich seems to be trembling. "She was such a sweet baby, looked just like me."

I take another bite, once again hardly chewing before I swallow the meat. "It's always difficult losing someone close to us." It feels like a platitude, but I know asking about her loss would be too intrusive and thus risky.

"Thank you," she says, letting the tears fall. "We'll make a new baby, though, another girl. She'll be just as cute as Jolene. Might hafta name her Jolene, too." She places the sandwich back on its plate and puts the plate on the floor, a few feet away. "Alright, no more tears, let's get to it."

She climbs on me, straddling me. She begins kissing me, which is the most intimate she's been, while grinding on me. I can tell it's what's bothering her that's causing her to be so

101

different, so affectionate. Not wanting to shun her or get in her bad graces, I kiss her back. Her lips are sweet and salty. She slips her tongue in my mouth and I caress her tongue with mine. I can feel my dick twitch with a jolt of blood but it doesn't react more than that, even though she's grinding on it. I can't stop seeing Ben staring at me, even with my eyes closed while we kiss. "You taste like her." I don't want to consider what that means. She looks down. "And you ain't even hard," she says, nearly in a sob.

"I'm sorry," I say, trying to think of something. "Maybe I'm just worn out from everything today. I'm sure I'll be better tomorrow."

"Mmhmm," she says with a sniffle and leaves. "Night," she says while turning off the light.

The sandwich is still next to me but I can't bring myself to attempt to retrieve it so that I can eat the rest of it. I would have to wriggle around and get my feet on it, then try to feed myself with my feet which is no small task given my weakened physical state.

I look across the room. Even with the light off, I can see Ben across the room, staring at me, leering. "You said you were going to get us out of here," Ben says, and a chill runs down my spine.

"Ben? I thought you were dead."

"Oh, duh, I am. I thought that was obvious."

I shudder. I'm not sure if Ben's voice is only occurring in my head or if he's really speaking. If the latter, either he's alive and fucking with me, or I'm speaking with a ghost, and I'm not ready for that. So, I don't engage.

"Oh, so you're going to ignore me now?" Across the pitch-black room, Ben stares at me. His eyes and toothy smile glow in the nonexistent light. "Don't leave me hangin', Daniel. Ha, ha, ha." His laugh is cold and mechanical. I can't see Ben's mouth move, but can only see his pale eyes and smile, which I know I shouldn't be able to see in the dark. "Well, I'll be right here when you're ready to talk." I look away and into the darkness to my right.

My migraine is making me feel nauseous, so I decide to save the rest of the sandwich for the morning, if I'm even able to sleep. With these migraines and no access to painkillers, there's no way of knowing. I start taking deep breaths, which helps enough to relax so that I edge on sleep, but just as I'm getting there, my headache comes roaring back and I'm fully awake.

Time drags. Moreso out of boredom than trying to escape, I find the pipe joint again and grip it between my hands. I twist as hard I can, but instead of rotating the joint, I scrape my palms against the ridges of the joint. Although I can't see it, I can tell I'm bleeding. Despite this, I continue, again gripping as hard as I can before I attempt even a fraction of a rotation on the pipe joint, but again I only succeed in scraping my palms further. They burn from the friction, but at the least the pain in my palms is taking my mind off the pounding headache. This time, I try using the rope for added grip and leverage, but this doesn't work and I end up punching myself in the back. I breathe in sharply through my nose, then grip the joint and try my damnedest to twist it, imagining I'm strangling the old man. It may be my imagination, but I believe I'm able to rotate it slightly, maybe a millimeter. I go to grab it again, but even just touching the pipe joint now is painful. I need to take a break and allow my hands to heal up a bit. I'll try again in the morning, which I expect to be after my next conjugal visit. For now, all I can do is hope that my sleepiness becomes so great that it overtakes the migraine and I can catch a few winks.

19

Sam

I stay awake, not that I would have had an easy time falling asleep. I tried temporarily forgetting about Emma, emphasis on *temporarily*, to give myself a reprieve from the debilitating grief. But finding out I'd taken bites out of my child's meat—and *liked it* no less—completely broke me. If I hadn't thrown up most of it already, I would be trying to make myself purge from the thought alone.

I stay awake until the house becomes completely silent, then stay awake a bit longer, hoping that I'll catch the household while they are in a deep sleep, in case there's any noise. Once I feel comfortable with the timing, I press firmly on the headboard's left post. First, I gently slide it off the top nails. Then I push with all my strength, steadily with both my left wrist and my right fingerless palm. The wood of the post creaks against the nails securing it at the bottom of the bedframe and its own bending stress, but I keep pushing it and pushing it. I stop momentarily when I hear a distant creak elsewhere in the house, but then after another minute of silence, I continue. As I push, I can also feel the post becoming even looser, but only gradually, until—*BANG! BANG!*—the post comes off the bed and smacks against the wall while the corner of the bed drops to the floor.

"Fuck, fuck, fuck, fuck!" I whisper as I begin to panic. I bend at the waist to try at the ropes at my feet. My left hand is still tied to the bedpost, so I drag it on the floor as I lean forward. I feel dizzy and weak, completely unprepared for the physical exertion I'm already putting on myself. I hear a door open somewhere else in the house and then footsteps.

There's no possible way I can untie my feet before the person approaching reaches the door, so I do my best to make the bed look like it did before. I pull my left arm toward me and am able to balance the post on its bottom. Then, I lean my bodyweight against the right side of the bed, bringing the left side up, teetering. I'm terrified that it doesn't look convincing at all. If the old man sees me like this, I just know that he'll "punish" me again. I need to make it appear like nothing happened in this room and I'm still asleep. I hear the footsteps come right up to the door and the locks being undone, slowly, methodically.

The door creaks open and a man stands in the doorway —a very big man who takes up the entire doorframe. He simply stands in the doorway, staring directly at me. His size is horrifying. My eyes are half-lidded so I can see without them appearing open, and though this is my first time seeing this man, I know who he is. This is the man who killed Emma. This must be the brother that Krystal mentioned.

His eyes glisten in the moonlight shining into the hallway in which he's standing. Though I can see where his eyes are, the hall is too dark for me to read his expression. I can only assume that he's not happy. His shoulders are broad and based on silhouette alone he appears not to have a neck. His arms are meaty and hang loosely at his sides, reminding me of a gorilla. He appears to be naked and erect. Even in the dark I can see his cock is massive. He continues staring at me in silence, which would make me believe that he couldn't see me in the dark room if it didn't seem obvious that his eyes were pointing directly at me. He arrived so quickly after the noise that he seems poised to strike. Whether he would just injure me, murder me, rape me, or all of the above, it's impossible to tell. His erection seems to indicate the worse of the possible incomes. As if confirming this, the big man grabs his erection and begins stroking it.

"You woke me up," he says. His voice is deep and a bit

slurred. I don't know if I should respond and apologize, or if I should go on pretending that I'm asleep and the sound didn't come from this room. The man is silent for a long moment, before again speaking. "Why'd you wake me up?"

I decide that the man might not leave me alone if I go on pretending that I'm asleep. "I'm sorry," I say gently. "I had a nightmare and I must have startled."

The man seems to chew on what I said for a while before replying, "What is star-dead?" He's still slowly stroking his erection, almost mindlessly.

I realize the man isn't drunk but developmentally disabled. Disabled or not, he's still a threat. I try to speak politely and calmly. At best, he's peeved. I wouldn't want to enrage him further. "The nightmare made me... jump awake."

The man thinks for a minute then says, "Nightmares are scary."

"They are," I say patiently. The man continues to stare at me. I don't want the conversation to continue any further, and despite the innocence of the conversation, I am scared shitless of this hulking man. After all, he's a murderer. If he's willing to kill an infant, he assuredly is perfectly capable of murdering a woman, or worse. On top of that, his looming stature is intimidating and he's jerking off, and I'm completely helpless while still mostly tied to the bed. Without thinking, I adjust my leg slightly, really all I can do with them, and the bed sways, which I quickly correct before it falls to the floor again. I can't see his face but I gauge his reaction to see if he notices. It's hard to say.

The man remains frozen in place and I wonder if he's actually sleepwalking. "My name's Sam," I say, in as friendly of a tone as I can muster.

"No," he says. He stops stroking himself. "The bunnies don't get names." I'm confused, but don't know what to say to ask for clarification. "I'm goin' back to bed now. Don't wake me up again." He stalks off, leaving the door fully ajar. After his footsteps recede into the house and I hear his door shut, I release the breath which I had not realized I had been holding.

Quietly, carefully, I ease the corner of the bed back to the floor. While the giant may not have noticed anything wrong, the old man or Krystal almost certainly would. Considering the unusual punishments the old man doles out for such minor offenses as accidentally getting my hand free or not wanting an old man to suckle on my breast so shortly after my child was murdered, I don't want to imagine what he would have in store for me for this offense.

I slowly lean forward, making no noise as I softly drag the loosened bedpost along the floor, lifting it as much as I can with my weakened arm. With my right palm, I hold one part of the rope on my left ankle while the fingers of my left hand get to work pulling the rope loose. It comes apart surprisingly quickly considering how much trouble the knots on my left wrist gave me. With one leg freed, I get to work on my right ankle, bringing the bedpost across my lap so that my left hand can reach the other side. It, too, comes free quickly and I nearly squeal in delight.

I carefully swing my legs over to the side of the crooked bed, nearly sliding off, but I maintain my balance. The last thing I want to do is wake up the brother again, or worse, the others. I bring the bedpost tied to my wrist to my teeth in an effort to pull the knot loose as I've done with many knots throughout my life when they were too tight to pull apart with my fingers. I can't discern if the rope moves at all and the anxiety fluttering in my stomach pushes me to just let it be for now. I'll bring it with me and sort it out after I first get as far away from this house as I can.

I stand for the first time in days. Every muscle in my body aches from the few days of atrophy along with the strain I more recently put my body through in my effort to escape. My knees buckle and my vision sways. To my benefit, my eyes are adjusted to the darkness of the room, so the added light from the hallway makes my environment clear enough for me to move around. I lift the bedpost across my body and hold it to myself with my right palm, like how a marching soldier would carry a rifle. Gingerly, I slip through the doorway, careful not to bump the bedpost on the doorframe as I exit.

I see the house outside the room for the first time and am not surprised much by the layout. The floors are a dusty hardwood which look like they've not been maintained. In the hallway is a sideboard table with a framed photo of a stern-faced woman. There's also a vase with flowers that have long dried into potpourri. Ahead, there are at least three other doors, maybe more as the hallway is blanketed in darkness at its end. I assume these are bedrooms, bathrooms, and closets. One of these rooms may contain my clothes and my phone, but I decide that these items are not worth the risk of waking someone up. Before traversing the hallway, I turn and quietly shut the bedroom door behind me, then twist all four locks. I want to get as much of a head start as possible before those creeps start looking for me, so making my room look undisturbed may buy me hours of precious lead time.

I walk quietly, padding on the front halves of my feet. My legs are sore from disuse and beg me to stop and rest, but I push onward. As I make my way through the hallway, the floor creaks, seemingly loudly in the otherwise silent house. I freeze, listening for the sound of someone waking up. If I hear someone approaching, I'll make a mad dash for where I believe the front door to the house to be and dash out, but if not, I'll remain as quiet as possible. After no respondent sound occurs, I continue.

Halfway through the hallway is an opening on my left leading to a dining room adjoining a kitchen. Surprisingly, these rooms look relatively clean, with no dirty dishes on the table or in the sink. I expected to see rotting food on the table and an overflowing trashcan, or blood and gore everywhere like a movie slaughterhouse. Really any kind of indication of a family gone mad, but instead everything's neat and tidy in here.

I glance around the table and the kitchen counter for anything that may be of some use to me, discovering a knife block. I pass a large avocado green refrigerator, which is old and hums very loudly. As I pass the behemoth, I feel a sense of dread. I can sense Emma's presence inside the fridge and want to look, to at the very least behold what's become of my baby. I can feel myself drawn to it, my hand reaching to the handle. But I worry that the sight alone will either cause me to collapse uselessly onto the floor, or scream, waking the entire household. I continue past the fridge.

I reach for the largest knife in the block and bump my bedpost on the edge of the counter, causing a quiet thump. I freeze in terror, ears perked and listening for movement from the direction of the bedrooms. I'm not breathing and my heart is pounding to the point I can hear my heartbeat. Outside, there are night sounds, the very same crickets or frogs I'd started getting accustomed to in my closed-off bedroom. I hear nothing else.

With my fingerless right palm, I lift the bedpost to a higher angle up to my ruined chest, then swing my left hand over again to grab a knife. As I guessed, it's a large cleaver, which is exactly what I want. Knife in hand, I slowly lower the post as I back away from the counter. Beyond the kitchen is the front door, my final destination. I dare not explore the house further, in fear of stumbling across another family member or a sleeping dog.

I don't realize my error of grabbing a knife until I reach the front door of the house. The door is locked and deadbolted, but even if it weren't, I don't know how I would twist the knob with my fingerless right hand while my left hand is gripping the knife. I don't want to just leave the knife here so I attempt to pass it to my other hand. I slide my right palm up the length of the bedpost, multiple splinters sliding into my palm one at a time. The distribution of weight is off and I nearly drop the bedpost onto the floor, so I stop my movement and take it more slowly. I pin the bedpost to my body with my right elbow and am able to take the knife from my left hand, first holding the knife handle between my hands, then sliding it down with my right palm until I'm pinning it to the board. Feeling clever for having worked this out, I reach my left hand down to open the locks, slowly and quietly as I've done with everything else so far. They click open easily, seeming to be newish, well-oiled locks. Finally, I open the door, which creaks. It doesn't creak loud enough to wake anyone, at least not compared to the other noises I've made so far.

I start to slide the knife back up to my left hand so that I can hold the post more firmly and the cleaver slips from my grip, plummeting down in a spin. Its point lands in the center of my right foot.

I'm able to hold back a scream, though tears blur my vision. *Of course*, I think. *I was having far too much luck for this not to happen.* Instead of reaching down to grab the knife, I slip out the door noiselessly and find myself on a wooden front porch which has a rocking chair shaking in the wind and homemade glass bottle wind chimes tinkling. I gently shut the door, then retrieve the knife out of my foot. A fresh line of blood drips out and the new wound feels like a papercut. Biting my lower lip to keep myself quiet through all the pain, I tiptoe down the porch steps and look around. A fall wind blows, chilling the house's residual warmth from my skin, a stark reminder of my nudity.

The porchlight is off and the only light I have is the moon. At a glance I can tell that the house is nowhere near the rest of society. The driveway leading up to the house is mostly dirt with sparse gravel and scattered crabgrass. Parked in the driveway is the pickup which I recognize from the night I was kidnapped. There's a possibility that the old man left his keys in the vehicle, but if memory serves, this truck is far too loud to operate without waking everyone in the house. Also, I can safely assume that the truck has a manual transmission and I don't know the first thing about driving stick.

In just about every direction are woods, with the narrow gravel driveway winding down the hill in front of me. The front yard is mostly overgrown with weathered ornamentation including several mossy lawn gnomes, flamingos, and a broken birdbath. My first thought is to take the driveway down until I find a road, however far an actual road may be, but that will likely be the first place they look, and it's not like I can hope to find someone driving around in such a secluded area at this hour. Hoping to choose the path least likely followed, I walk around to the back of the house.

Behind the house, I'm surprised to discover a cornfield. Tall stalks, perhaps twelve feet tall, tower over me. More than half seem to be producing corn, while others appear to be dead but still standing. Between the rows are many weeds, some half as tall as the corn, creating a thicket. The moon does a poor job of lighting the interior of the cornfield, so I can only see a few feet ahead of me. This almost seems to be too perfect, so I enter, turning my body sideways to compensate for the bedpost I'm carrying.

Leaves from both cornstalks and weeds brush against my body as I make my way through the tucked away field. Corn also rubs against me, which feels like fingers or hands brushing along my shoulders and arms. Some of the leaves are thick and scratch at me, but compared to the pain in my hand, breast, and foot, the scratches are nothing. As I make my way through the cornfield, pale moonlight dances through the stalks, casting ominous shadows. I swear I see a tall figure moving between the rows but chalk it up to it being a play of the light coupled with my overactive imagination, which itself can be blamed on a culmination of sleep deprivation, starvation, dehydration, and let's not forget the ever-present trauma to which I keep receiving new additions.

The earth is dry beneath my feet, the ground covered with weeds and fallen corn leaves. Every so often, I step on a corncob in its husk and nearly roll my ankle. After much walking, I find a small gap in the cornfield where the dead corn must have broken and composted into the earth. I decide this will be as good a spot as any to free myself from the bedpost so that I can cover more ground, more quickly. I seat myself on the ground cross-legged, which also affords me a closer look at my newly-wounded foot.

In the moonlight, the blood looks black, but at least it looks like the bleeding has halted. I drop the knife in the dirt in front of me, figuring it would be easier to pick up from the ground than to try to pass it to myself again. As I reach for the knife with my fingerless palm, hoping to hook it in my wrist, I spy a small pile of shucked corn, maybe twenty or so in total, some of which gnawed down to the cob. I assume some sort of animal must have done this since people don't eat uncooked corn, even people as crazy as those who live here. I'm able to pick up the knife, pinching it between my palm and forearm, tucking it in my right wrist, but when I go to saw at the rope binding my left wrist to the bedpost, the knife quickly slips out of my grasp. Fortunately, this time it doesn't pierce me.

I look around for a new approach, but don't see anything sparking an idea. I could possibly tuck the knife into a cornstalk, but it wouldn't hold the knife any better than my mangled hand. I then remember seeing a documentary-style TV series featuring a person born without arms, who did everything with her feet. Or maybe she was in a horrible accident and lost her arms, which I can relate to. I grab the knife handle in the arches of my feet and lean forward to press the rope against the knife. I'm able to saw the cleaver against the rope, causing it to fray. I find that bending forward and backward gives more strength to the cuts than trying to do it by bringing my feet forward and back, though the latter has more control, so I combine approaches. Soon, the rope has frayed to the point that I can just pull it apart with my right palm. The rope and bedpost both fall to the ground, softly onto the earth, and for the first time in days, I feel free. However, I don't want to dwell here so close to the house for long, so I pick up the knife and walk onward, estimating a direction that's away from the house.

The cornfield is much smaller than I've seen in movies, though I wouldn't expect Iowa or Kansas-sized cornfields in the mountains of Kentucky, where I believe myself to be. The cornfield gives way to tall brush before a more forested area, which I go into without pause. I forget about the cut on the top of my foot as each step through the forest stabs and pokes at my bare soles. Thorns and brambles scratch against my arms and cold wind chills my bones, also causing my sole remaining nipple to stiffen to ice. It's freezing cold, maybe below freezing, with the wind exacerbating the chill. I hadn't realized how much the thick cornfield had been keeping me warm until I left its embrace.

With each step I take, leaves crackle and twigs snap. I can hear distant wildlife scatter, scurry, or otherwise relocate. It relieves me to hear that each noise seems to be moving away from me. The moon peeks through the trees somewhat better than the cornstalks, or at least differently. The forest ahead quickly fades into a gray-blue obscurity, though. I grew up in the suburbs with few trees scattered throughout my neighborhood. I have no prior experience being in the woods. Being naked and alone only amplifies my feeling of vulnerability. Getting increasingly cold, I hug myself, careful to point the knife outward. I focus on the way ahead, though there is no path. While doing so, I trip on a root sticking out of the ground and spill into a thorny bush, dropping the knife.

"Ah, fuck," I whisper. Even though I've travelled a good distance from the house, I don't trust how noise may carry and refrain from screaming though I wish I could. I pull myself backward out of the thorns slowly, attempting to minimize the amount of scratching they do. The scratches on my burned chest hurt worse, feeling as though I've re-opened this wound. For a long moment, I kneel in front of the bush, quietly sobbing. The pain is dizzying, causing me to be lightheaded. Every time I think things are going well, I receive another setback. It just seems as though the universe wants to torture me, like this is some sort of trial with absolutely no payoff, except possibly survival. But without Emma, how does survival even matter?

I sniffle once more and begin to peer in the bush hoping for a glint of the knife, but it's too dark. I'm forced to reach inside the bush blindly with my remaining hand and feel around. The thorns scratch me as I paw around beneath the bush. Finally, I find it and triumphantly grab it, inadvertently grabbing the sharp end of the knife which slices into the inside of my left palm. I squeak in pain and release the knife, then find its handle and retrieve it. *Just another excruciating wound to add to the tally*, I think miserably. I suck in air through my teeth and stand, knife in hand, ignoring the fresh blood leaking out of my hand. I'm surprised I haven't run out of blood yet, with everything I've gone through recently. I still feel weak and light-headed but am hoping my adrenaline will push me through all of this until I get somewhere relatively safe.

To my right, and extremely close, I hear a large branch snap. I halt again, holding the knife at the ready. My first thought is that the old man found me, but this doesn't make sense. Up until this point, I haven't heard any noise aside from what I took to be small animals moving around or the wind, nothing physically large. If I were followed by the old man or anyone else from the house, I would have known much sooner than this, so it must be an animal or maybe branches just randomly fall off the trees from time to time. Who knows? I try to see through the branches as best I can but with the minimal light and great amount of foliage across vast distances in every direction, there really is no way to tell the difference between a bush and an animal standing still. Aside from random acorns falling from nearby trees and insects buzzing or chirping, the forest is silent.

Keeping my eyes in the direction of the sound, I continue

moving in the direction I was heading. When I hear a twig snap, I stop again, but don't wait as long this time, realizing the sound may have been another small animal flitting away. I nearly walk headfirst into a tree, so I stop keeping such a close watch behind myself and instead just use my ears.

My legs feel like they're about to give out, so I stop to rest at a large, thick-barked oak. Before I sit beneath the tree, I use a foot to brush away the acorns and other objects from the base of the trunk. Once I have it about as comfortable as I can make it, I sit and rest my back on the tree, spreading my legs out in front of me. I set the knife down to get as good a look as I can at the cut on my hand in the moonlight. From what I can tell, it doesn't look very deep, though as I'm looking, I realize that even if it were, there's nothing I can really do about it. It's not like I have a shirt sleeve I can tear off and use as a bandage.

As long as I'm doing a self-assessment, I check my foot and find that all of the walking has opened the wound from the knife falling on it. I can see a slow stream of blood leaking down the side of my foot. The wound itself still feels like a papercut, which is no worse than my other injuries, including splinters which I can't see well enough to remove. My entire body is also sore from the physical exertion with a lack of nutrients. My throat is dry and scratchy from dehydration. Despite all of the pain, I am exhausted enough to fall asleep, but I know I can't yet. It's still nighttime and I need to put as much distance between myself and the house as possible before daybreak.

Pushing on my knees for leverage, I stand, my knees popping loudly. I groan when I realize that I left the knife on the ground and have to bend down to pick it up. Fortunately, I can see where it's at so I don't need to paw around again, risking another hand injury. I nearly stumble from bending over, but am able to right myself before this happens.

Since I left the cornfield, I've been going primarily uphill, which is unlikely to bring me closer to any sort of civilization, but this is also good in that it's a clear way of getting me away from the house. I can't get turned around so long as I continue uphill. However, shortly after leaving the tree where I rested, it's hard to tell if I'm going up or downhill. I believe this means that I'm cresting the hill or mountain or whatever I've been climbing, but this is concerning since I'm afraid I got turned around and may inadvertently start heading back toward the house. I can't see far enough in any direction to get some sort of landmark and everything looks the same as it has for the past indeterminable amount of time. I'm lost, which isn't as troubling for me as it would be under normal circumstances, because even starving to death is better than what's waiting for me at that house.

I can only hope that the direction I'm walking in is at least close to a continuation of where I've been heading as the terrain starts sloping downward. I walk for what feels like hours, the moon changing position perceptibly. The longer I walk, the more comfortable I feel that I'm not heading back to where I started. The wind picks up again, so I begin walking more swiftly, hoping to get my blood flowing as a means of keeping warm, while keeping my eyes ahead so I don't run into a tree or thorny bush again.

My progress again abruptly stops when I hear high-pitched yapping and howling to my left, some distance away. Though I've never heard such sounds before, I'm fairly certain they're coyotes based on how high-pitched the sounds are compared to what I've heard wolves sound like, again basing this on my experience from television and movies. I'm not sure if the sounds mean they have seen me and are hunting me or if it's unrelated to my presence. I stand at the ready with the knife gripped tightly, anticipating an attack at any moment. My heart is again pounding hard.

Eventually, the noise subsides. I have no way of knowing how loud coyotes are, or even for sure if it really were coyotes making the noise. I stay poised, my head and eyes turning this way and that, waiting for some other noise to indicate a wild animal or animals are approaching. After the silence stretches long enough that I believe myself to be safe, I resume walking in the general direction I've been heading, knife still at the ready just in case I'm mistaken.

Suddenly, I tumble forward, my ankle twisting on surprisingly steep terrain. I focus on gripping the knife while using my right arm to block my head and face from colliding into anything during my fall. I slide and roll down the leafy hill, scratching myself on surrounding plants and coming to rest on a floor of stones and pebbles. From the trickling sound I realize that it's a creek bed! Without hesitation, I drop the knife and crawl to the creek. I scoop up as much water as I can between my damaged hands, slurping up the cool water thirstily. The water tastes better than any water I've ever tasted. Its coolness emanates throughout my body, causing me to shiver while also feeling like it's healing me in some way, giving a tingling sensation. I feel as though my body is soaking the water up like a sponge. I only stop when I feel like I'm going to regurgitate from drinking it too fast. Once my stomach settles, I go back to scooping water and downing it until I feel full, not even so hungry anymore. With no idea what plants are safe to eat, it may be some time before I eat again.

Not wanting to feel lost anymore, I follow the creek downstream. I'm pleased to find that the earth beneath my feet is no longer rough and sharp, mostly covered in mud and easy to see stones. This makes travel go slower than the wooded area since I don't want to step wrong on a stone and twist my ankle, but the roundness of the stones and pebbles is better than the twigs, thorns, and acorns stabbing into my feet, legs, and arms. I also feel comforted by having a source of fresh water directly adjacent to me. I imagine this creek will lead to a river, which will in turn lead to a lake. People like to build houses next to lakes so I may be able to find someone who can help.

My weariness is weighing me down even more with all of the careful walking along stones. While I am thankful for the relatively smooth walking area, my feet are sore from having walked on stones for so long. Plus, the air coming off the water is frigid. Even at the snail's pace I must have as an average since I set out, I should have walked miles by now. My legs are very sore and ready for a long rest. Dawn is breaking, though I can't see the horizon, just a glow over the trees. I can't walk forever and will need to rest soon.

While it has been great having the stream as a landmark to ensure I continue to walk in the same general direction— at one point in the forest, I worried I was walking in circles —I know that it's too open of a place to sleep, so I cross the stream and go into the woods on the other side. I know not to wander too far from the stream. I want to be able to easily find it again when I wake up, so I periodically look behind myself to ensure I can still see and hear the water. Soon, I find a small group of trees, surrounded by a large-leafed bush, providing an appropriate amount of cover while still allowing me to see out. I slip between the trees and jab my knife in the ground close enough that I can easily grab it without risking rolling onto it while asleep. I brush away as many sticks and acorns as I can to make my "bed" as comfortable as possible. I breathe a heavy sigh of relief and allow myself to fall into a deep, dreamless sleep.

20

Krystal

I'm horny which I guess should be no surprise considerin' how much dick I been gettin' lately, and not just any ol' piddly country boy pecker like I was getting in school but a big ol' city boy black dick, three times a day. No more goin' in the field with the corn for me! At least not for the time bein'. Before I even roll outta bed I got myself all slick thinkin' about ridin' that basement bunny boy. Got myself rubbin' my thighs together, all hot 'n' bothered, ready to go on downstairs right away!

First things first, I need some coffee and I'm half-starved, so breakfast would be nice. Grandaddy is already up, as usual, fixin' up some slices of bunny boy leg. On the cutting board, he's got a thigh which he's waxed all the hair off. Grandaddy must get up mighty early to be doin' all this work just for breakfast. But he ain't got nothin' else to do since he ain't got no job, not that he needs one after sellin' all that land he got from *his* Grandaddy. Most of the land Grandaddy hunts on used to be his but he don't mind, he still hunts there as if it's still his. So, he's got the thigh just sittin' there on the cutting board all cleaned up lookin' good. It don't have much fat in it, prob'ly on account of it comin' from a soldier boy who was too skinny for my tastes, but I'm sure his meat's still good. Smells good anyway while Grandaddy throws it on the pan. While it's cookin', he wraps up the meat he ain't sliced yet with tinfoil and puts it in the fridge next to what's left of Jolene. He musta had Big Joe move the other leg to one of the freezers cause I don't see it in the fridge. It really is too much meat to try and eat it in the next few days before it starts to go

119

bad. That's why we usually only take a bit off the bunnies at a time so as to keep the meat fresh, but of course soldier bunny boy got to rough with his legs like a damn spider cricket.

He fixes us up some thigh meat and eggs, one of them good ol' Southern meals that just warm ya to yer core. Big Joe is still sleepin' so we get to have breakfast by ourselves. "Gettin' mighty cold out," Grandaddy says, gnawing on his food. His dentures jostle around in his mouth. He must not've set 'em in yet.

I light up a cigarette, havin' finished my meal and nod. I say, "We sure as shit got enough meat to pull us through the winter but we might need to go get some groceries for bread and everything else. I could use another carton of cigarettes, too."

"Yep," Grandaddy says. "We can go this afternoon. I was goin' to have some milk with breakfast." Grandaddy laughs to himself. It takes me a second to realize he's talkin' about the bunny bitch's titty milk.

"That's fine," I say, sipping my coffee. "I was just fixin' to fuck my basement bunny boy."

"Don't let me keep ya," Grandaddy says with a sneer, still eatin' his breakfast. I smile and bring my cigarette with me when I go downstairs.

I'm all excited again! I mean my pussy feels like it's just *drippin'* wet which I think means I got an egg ready and just need the boy cum to turn it into a baby. I run down the basement stairs and there's my fuckboy just starin' off at his buddy like he's dead or something, but he's still blinkin' and breathin' so my boy bunny ain't dead. I'm wonderin' if they might really be gayboys after all, the way they're just lookin' at each other. Whatever floats their little gay boat, I guess. All I know is I can still get my bunny to cum when I need it so I start suckin' on my bunny boy to get him hard and it just ain't workin'. Best I can do is get it halfway there but it's still pretty much just a limp noodle in my hand. He's just starin' off past me, his eyes lookin' all tired like he ain't slept all night. I give him a little slap on the cheek to try to wake him up and he looks at me all slow but his face don't change. His eyes are as red as a dog's dick. I huff and am about to pout but then I get an idea and run off.

I get up to the kitchen when I run into Grandaddy.

"It's the bitch!" Grandaddy says and he goes runnin' from the kitchen to his room. I don't know what he's talkin' 'bout so I go to the Bunny Room and she ain't there! The bed is all broke and one of the bedposts is missin', so she must've brought it with her. As I come out, I hear him shout from his room as if I might still be in the kitchen, "The bitch is gone! You mind the house! Me and Big Joe gonna go fetch her!"

I go back to the kitchen and see there's some thigh meat still sittin' on the cutting board, though Grandaddy put most of it back in the fridge so I slice some off and fry it up to make some sandwiches for Grandaddy and Big Joe to take with 'em in case they're gone all day. I love the smell of thigh meat cookin' almost as much as I love the taste.

Pretty soon Grandaddy comes back out of his room to fetch Big Joe and tell him to get his clothes on, that "We goin' huntin'" and sure enough, Grandaddy's got on his huntin' gear, his old faded cammy pants and jacket that he got from the Army surplus store some years ago, and he's got his rifle slung over his back. I get the sandwiches I made for them and wrap 'em up in tinfoil. Big Joe comes out wearing just a t-shirt and jeans and Grandaddy says "That'll have to do, put on your boots. We're goin' to drag that bitch back here. And when we do, she's really gonna get it now."

I give Grandaddy the sandwiches and he gives me a kiss on the cheek. His beard is all tickly as it's always been, one thing I love about Grandaddy. Big Joe looks like he might still be asleep while he shoves his boots on. He asks me to tie them for him since he can't never remember how and I oblige since Grandaddy's right there waiting. They leave and I lock the door.

121

We always keep the door locked.

I have some ideas for my bunny boy, but first I gotta clean everything up in the kitchen. Grandaddy drilled it in us that it's super important to keep our kitchen clean. He knows that if Johnny Law ever comes sniffin' 'round here, it wouldn't do to have a bloody, messy kitchen. Once I'm done, I head outside.

When I get outside, it's as cold as a witch's titty and I'm wearin' nothin' but my panties. *Whatever,* I think, *it won't take me but a minute.* I go runnin' 'round back to the field. When I get there, I can hear Grandaddy talkin' to Big Joe. He's callin' him an idiot or something and they're real far off in the cornfield, maybe even just past it in the woods. When I look on the ground, I see why they're over here. There's little bloody footprints, just the right foot, leadin' right into the cornfield, so that musta been where the girl bunny done ran off to. I'm sure she left all sorts of tracks and markers to make it real easy for Grandaddy to track her down. If he can track a deer, he sure as shit can track some stupid bunny. Lord knows how she got out, but I'm sure they'll find her soon enough. Grandaddy's got his rifle and he's a mighty good shot so he can get her in the leg so she can't run no more and Big Joe can carry her all the way back home. Grandaddy will probably take her legs for this, which means we'll be eatin legs for a month or two between her and the other basement bunny boy.

One time we had us a whole family of bunnies, a Momma bunny, a Daddy bunny, and a little kid bunny, and we took their legs off at the knees and their arms at the elbows and then we didn't have to tie them up no more. All three of 'em was in the Bunny Room together. They could just walk around the bedroom on all fours like they was some cows. One time I walked in on the Daddy bunny fuckin' the Momma bunny while they was cows and that was one of the funniest things I ever did see! The kid cow was in the room just sleepin' on the bed like nothin' was happenin'! Of course, I woke the kid cow-bunny up and told the Momma and Daddy cow-bunnies to keep at it so he could watch 'em too! I don't think he knew what was goin' on.

Anyway, I don't need to go in the field to fetch what I need. I get up on my tippy toes and find a nice sized corn and pluck it from its stalk. I start huskin' it on the way back to the front of the house, just singin' to myself, "Jimmy cracked corn and I don't care," pullin off the leaves and the corn strings.

I know I mentioned before that I got a smart phone and I got the Internet, and that's because we need some way to see the cameras in the woods and you can get a fancy phone from just about any store these days real cheap, and you just buy the minutes. Anyway, sometimes I use it to look up pornos just because it's fun to watch. I don't need 'em when I do my business in the cornfield since I can just think about my soaps boys and that does the trick, though I gotta admit the pornos will get me all drippy between the legs and I'll find myself either rubbin' my clit or runnin' outside to fetch me a corncob. On one of the pornos I done seen, the girl in it did something that stuck with me and got me curious if it would work in real life, so that's where I got my idea I'm fixin' to try.

21

Daniel

I don't sleep, at least not that I can tell. My entire head is aching like it's about to pop, which would be a blessing if it did truly burst. On top of this, I've started having tremors again, similar to seizures but I can still see during them and remember everything afterward. When the light comes on, I realize I've been staring at Ben all night in the dark, and Ben has been staring right back. There's a large black fly on Ben's left eye, probably feasting. Ben's mouth doesn't move but I can hear him say, "Wish you were here."

I remember during what was likely the night hearing a loud bang above, which I took to be someone falling, but it could have been that big man stomping because I'm sure I hear heavy footsteps directly afterward. I strain to twist the pipe joint again and it moves a millimeter at most. My hand is raw.

Second, minutes, hours later, the light is on. Someone must have turned it on, they must have. It doesn't turn on by itself, unless it does. I wonder how long it will be before the big black fly is able to work itself into Ben's eye. Has it already punctured the surface and is now drinking the fluid underneath with its probiscis like a straw? Maybe it will tunnel through somehow and come out the other eye. I watch Ben's eye to see if it goes flat, or leaks out. Ben stares back, still smiling. *Wish you were here.*

More flies have lit on Ben's bloody stumps, what remains of his legs. Part of a long tribal tattoo was cut off halfway. I swear I can see Ben's fingers move, as if adjusting, or maybe scratching.

His arms are still bound above his head, just like mine.

There's noise on the stairs. *Are they checking on me?* I don't look, don't care to look. I can hear someone moving around above me, and someone else on the stairs. The girl is back, probably wanting to get more of my seed. That's all I'm good for now, the only reason I'm alive. I wish I were dead like Ben, *wish I were there.* The girl plays around with my dick, but I've lost a lot of sensation, and nothing about what she does is sexy anymore, if it ever were to begin with. *How long before the old man joins in again?* I think dismally. *Did she notice that Ben's dead?* It doesn't seem like it. I can no longer feel sadness over Ben's death, though I'm sure I'm still grieving. Hell, I could be grieving Ben's death or my own impending death. *At least the headache is subsiding, for now.* She slaps me, which wakes me up a bit, enough to look at her anyway. I'm so tired. Now that the headache is calming down, it's time to sleep. *Won't she let me sleep?*

As if on command, she leaves me there, though she leaves the light on. *That's okay*, I think, *I can fall asleep with the light on, I've done it before.* I try closing my eyes, but I still see Ben, just as clear as when my eyes were open. I look back to the pile of boxes just to have something to look at besides Ben's slow disintegration. I notice several boxes piled on top of each other, all with the same phrase written on them. "Bunny Pelts." *What a weird thing to store in boxes*, I think. My head is foggy. The word bunny seems to mean something more, I just can't put my finger on it. I look back to Ben, past Ben, *through* Ben.

What feels like seconds later, the girl comes back. *She won't let me sleep until I give her what she wants.* I give her my attention and allow her to move my body. One at a time, she slides my feet up to my ass, then pushes at both of my ankles, pressing my back against the pipe. I think this to be strange, since before she would just leave me as is, suck me and fuck me, then leave.

I think my eyes must be playing tricks on me again

because she starts fucking herself with an ear of corn. She's in a similar position as me, seated on the floor facing me with her legs spread and knees up. She holds up the top half of her body on her left elbow and with her right hand, she guides the ear of corn in and out of her pussy. It's strange enough to wake me out of my fugue, and oddly, my cock twitches with excitement. It makes a wet slurping sound as she moves the corn in and out. Then, she pulls the corn out and it's slick with her juices. Her hand goes low again and I don't realize what she's doing until I feel the pressure pushing against my asshole. She puts her knees on my feet to hold them in place, though I'm too afraid to move now, afraid that if I lean forward, it will be worse. With my back literally to the wall, I can't move away. She pushes the corncob into my ass deeply—there's a sharp pain—she rotates it, then slides it back out slowly before shoving it back in. She's looking down at what she's doing, her face a smirk. She's clearly enjoying it. The corn feels like a spike in my ass. The closest thing I ever felt to this before was when I had taken a shit that seemed to be too big that hurt when it came out. This is far worse. She keeps going in and out, grinning like the devil, like Ben. Strangely, a heat starts growing from my core and I realize that she's using the corncob to massage my prostate. My cock starts growing despite my misgivings and she uses her free hand to start stroking me. She strokes my cock at the same speed and rhythm as she's pistons the cob in my ass. I can feel the individual hard pieces of corn still on the uncooked cob rubbing against my anus.

As soon as my dick is as hard as she wants it to be, she stops pushing the corn in my ass, just leaving it there, pulls a few rubber bands from her wrist and wraps them around the base of my cock, twisting them both around three times to create an even tighter makeshift cock ring than last time. My cock is already purple from the blood trapped inside. She jumps on top of me, knocking my knees down and feet forward with her small, bony ass, and easily slides down my length. She starts rocking against me wildly, feverishly. Her pussy is hot and sopping wet, making squishing and smacking noises as she grinds on me. I can feel her juices dripping down my balls and ass crack.

Another tremor rocks through me and I feel like I'm losing my breath. My vision blurs and goes whitish but I never lose sight. "Wow, a human vibrator!" the girl says, not slowing her rocking. Eventually, the tremors subside. I know that if I ejaculate in her, she will leave me alone, at least for a few hours, which will give me a chance to sleep. So, I focus on how good it feels to have her gripping me. While I don't like the pain from getting fucked in the ass by an ear of corn, the pressure on my prostate seems to be increasing the pleasure I feel on my dick. Soon enough, I spurt inside her and though I hate myself for it, it feels fantastic. She continues riding me, milking every drop of cum out of me. Then she collapses on her back, lying between my legs, tilting her hips up to hold my seed inside her.

"I can feel it," she says. The post-coital slumber is dragging me under and I welcome it. Whatever the girl is saying seems secondary until she says, "I'm pregnant!" There's no way she can know this now, but she seems to sincerely believe it. I don't care. I'm even glad. *Maybe she'll let me go now,* I think then almost laugh. I'm drifting off to sleep again when she speaks. "Oh my gawd, your ass done ate the corn!"

That wakes me right the fuck up. I panic and look down, hoping I'll still see it, maybe on the ground now and out of my ass, but it's not there. She's looking at my asshole as if waiting for the corn to poke back out. "I'm sure it'll come back eventually. You'll just have a *really* corny shit soon." She laughs as if this is the funniest thing in the world. "Anyway, now that I'm good and knocked up, I can finally eat that pretty cock of yours." I'm confused, even when she puts me in her mouth. I think she's just there to suck me off again. I feel like I can fall asleep again, so I let my heavy eyes flutter closed.

My eyes pop open when the blonde brings her incisors together just below the head of my cock. My headaches and the pain in my ass are nothing compared to this. I try to move away but I can't. My entire body is too weak to put up enough of a fight to do anything more than wriggle beneath her. She turns her head so that her molars are mashing on the head, which she chews on like a dog would a bone. Her teeth squeak against my dick. With each time she gnaws on my dick, a sharp pain shoots up through my abdomen. I lose sensation in my arms and legs and nearly faint from the amount of pain, but each bite also brings me back to full consciousness. She switches to the other side of her mouth and I hear a loud smacking pop, though the pain feels no different than the other times she chewed. I can't help but look down and watch in horror as she eats. The pop apparently was her breaking through my flesh. The head of my dick looks as though it's burst a seam and blood is now shooting out like a thin geyser. The girl doesn't seem to mind, letting the blood cover her face, her eyelids closing to not let any get in her eyes. She bites down hard with her incisors, breaking through the connective tissue between the head of my dick and the shaft. More blood shoots out, but the stream has weakened and now seeps out lazily. She runs her tongue along the length, lapping the blood off my dick like a delicacy, but there's far too much for her to get it all. She then takes me in her mouth, all the way to the base, deep-throating me. There's nothing sensual about it, though, as she bites on the base of my dick hard, but not hard enough to break the skin. She moves back up to the top of me, scraping her teeth up, and bites hard again, this time severing the head of my dick from the shaft. She loudly chews on it with her mouth open, the flesh squeaking and squelching as her teeth grind it into a mash. She chews and chews like it's a too-big piece of gum, moving the flesh between each side of her mouth, which I can see resting in each of her cheeks when she does this. Strangely, madly, she's still stroking me as if trying to make me cum, but really just milking more and more blood out of me. She swallows my chewed-up dick head, then bends back down for more, to take another bite. She bites into me quickly this time, severing another piece of my dick about an inch down from where my head was. The pain isn't new to the sharp, screaming pain coming from my crotch. Her lips smack and she chews this new piece of me, masticating it as if thoughtfully savoring the difference in flavor between my head and the flesh of my shaft. She swallows and takes a third bite, this time bigger than the bite before. She chews this piece more quickly. When she swallows, I can see the piece of me moving down her throat into her esophagus.

She takes a break from my mangled cock to put one of my balls in her mouth. She bites down on my scrotum and rips it open with her teeth, then pulls it off me. She slurps my scrotum flesh like spaghetti, then chews it while holding and eyeing my now exposed testicles. The pain is deep—I can feel it in my stomach—when she pulls at them with her hand, trying to free them from my body. She gives up on this and bends over to bite them off of me with her incisors as she's done with the rest of my manhood. She eats one nut at a time, the first one popping between her teeth openly, squirting a combination of pearly white semen, the brown flesh of the testicle, and the bright red blood coating it, the spray landing across my face. "Mmm," she says with pleasure, then pops the other nut in her mouth like it's a snack during a movie.

Her hands and arms are covered in blood and viscera up to the elbow. Her face is still covered in blood from the spray and the blood has made its way down her neck to her exposed breasts, drip-drip-dripping from her nipples. She rubs the blood around on her breasts, playing with her nipples as she savors my last testicle. She's breathing hard as if nearing orgasm. While still playing with herself, she takes one last bite of my dick at the base. It takes a few bites for her jaw to make it through the flesh, but she eventually succeeds and the rubber bands pops off into the air just as she moves her head back to chew on the last of me. She shudders with an orgasm.

She wipes her mouth with the back of her hand which only smears the blood around, and stands. "I have to say, you have the yummiest cock I have ever had. And your balls..." She pinches her fingers to her lips and pantomimes a chef's kiss. "That might be the hardest I ever came just now. Good night, bunny boy," she says, shutting off the light as she leaves.

I'm tremoring again, which I pray are death shakes which will take me quickly, but no such luck. Sleep doesn't come for me, but I do slip into unconsciousness nonetheless.

22

Jared

I'm a bit surprised when Sam hasn't called by the fourth day, but not worried. For the third night in a row, I've had Anna over, and as before, she stays in my bed, naked. It feels weird to call it my *and* Sam's bed, especially while she's away. She's done nothing to pay for the bed or the house that it's in. It's my house, my bed, my everything really. Even most of her clothes are mine, really. I bought them.

I do wonder why my wife hasn't called and am almost considering trying to call *her* again, maybe leave a message this time, but think better of it. To call her again would be playing her silly little game and losing it at that. No, eventually she'll cave and come crawling back to call me and say my favorite line: "I'm sorry for being such a bitch to you lately." I love when she acknowledges that she's irrational and that I'm the sane, calm, rational one who should be apologized to. I really work hard to keep her housed and clothed, to take care of the baby. For a moment, I have difficulty remembering the name of the baby. It wasn't the name I came up with. The name I came up with was for if she had a boy, which she didn't, so she got to name the baby. I do not look forward to the extra female hormones in the house or the likelihood that Sam and the girl will sync up their periods, making life hell for me.

When I discovered that I could get away with having Anna over while Sam is away, I took the week off from work, telling them I needed a bit of a break. And when I take a break, it's fine

OSCAR BRADY

for Anna to take a break since she's not needed in the office while I'm out. So, no one notices that both of us are gone for the week, and I'm sure no one will raise any eyebrows when we both come back at the same time next week.

We were caught once at the office. Anna was giving me a hand job in the stairway, which we had assumed no one used, at least not any of the fat asses we see in the office day to day. One of the male interns happened to use the stairs that day and nearly walked right into us. I fired him within the hour, stating that I caught him stealing office supplies and lying about it. The intern was stripped of his employee badge so he couldn't enter the building again and tell anyone about what he'd seen. I had also given the intern a thousand dollars to keep the whole matter quiet. From then on, Anna and I agreed that we should keep to ourselves while at work during normal work hours, and just get hotels during our lunch break if we wanted some midday fun. Otherwise, we could do whatever we wanted while "burning the midnight oil," and no one would be the wiser. Hotels were paid for with the company card, which no one checked the books on but me, so even Sam had no clue what was going on since I don't use any of our cards.

This morning, my phone finally rings, which I assume is Sam. It's her mom's number, so she must be using her mom's phone to call. *Maybe her phone is dead*, I think. She's always forgetting something, so it wouldn't surprise me if she forgot her phone charger, so now she's stuck in St. Louis with a dead phone. I stare delightedly at Anna's peach of an ass as I pick up. "Well, look who finally decided to call me back," I say.

"Hello?" It's Sam's mother's voice. "Is this Jared?" I can't believe Sam actually has her mother calling on her behalf. She could never fight her own battles, and her mother's enough of a bitch to do the fighting for the both of them.

"Yes, it's me, Lori. How can I help you?"

"I was just calling to see if Sam is there." I freeze. I believed

132

that Sam was with her mother. If she isn't with her, where is she? "She's not answering her phone and I've left six messages. Is she mad at me?" *Funny, Lori, I thought she was mad at* me. I wonder if Sam has been hiding out in a hotel somewhere, watching me. I shake my head as if shaking the thought out. It doesn't make sense. If she suspected anything, she surely would have caught me by now.

"No, she's not here. I thought she was with you."

"No, she's not with me." *No shit, idiot.* "Do you think something happened to her? Is Emma with you?"

I again temporarily forget the name of our daughter, then it hits me. "No, Sam brought the baby with her. Maybe she stopped somewhere because it got late. I'm sure she'll show up soon." It's been four days.

Sam's mother is silent for a minute, considering this. "I think it's best if we report her missing."

I slap my forehead. At the sound, Anna turns over, her breasts tumbling with her. She smiles up at me. She purses her lips and spreads her legs to show off her waxed-hairless pussy and beckons me with a finger. "Maybe you're right," I say into the phone, now rushed. "Don't worry, I'll do it. I'll go in and have them file the report. But still, I'm sure she'll turn up soon."

"Okay," Lori says. "Call me when it's done."

"Okay, will do. Bye," and I hang up before she can say anything else. I throw my phone down and crawl back into bed.

"Who was that?" Anna asks, kissing my chest.

"It was work. Don't worry about it, they can wait." I kiss her neck and am soon back inside her.

I wasn't lying to Sam's mother, though. I know that if I don't do something it will look bad on me. It's clear that my wife is missing, and a loving husband is supposed to be concerned and trying every avenue to get her back. I would be perfectly fine if she found somewhere else to live and isn't coming back. We're not happy. Sam has to be as aware as I am. Yes, I'll call the police and file a missing person report... eventually. First, I need to get Anna to go somewhere and I need to clean up the house before the cops come to ask questions which they're sure to do when I report Sam missing. I wish I could push this off on Sam's mother to do, but I know that would be even worse for me. I didn't do anything wrong, so I have nothing to worry about, but I just don't want the additional scrutiny.

Anna seems to drag her feet in getting ready to leave. She only brought a weekend bag. It's not like she brought a lot of stuff. She brought a change of clothes but hadn't had to use any clothes since arriving. She's mostly been naked around the house for me, something Sam would never do. Whenever she's left the bed for other parts of the house—say for a glass of water or wine—Anna would borrow Sam's robe then come back to the bed and be naked again. I consider how fulfilled I finally feel while I think about how Anna and I have had more sex in the last few days than Sam and I have had since she got pregnant. The few times I tried to make advances with Sam, she would turn away or say, "Not tonight, honey, I'm too tired from taking care of the baby." The baby was sapping her energy and I have my own needs which Sam hasn't been fulfilling. The affair isn't my fault if you consider all the factors.

After tidying the place and spraying it with some Febreze, I take a quick shower, then call the police's non-emergency number. "I'm just worried about my wife," I say. "Normally she doesn't go this long without answering her phone, and she's not even picking up for her mother." I explain that she was driving to see her mother and that she told me that she didn't want me to come, that I should focus on my work since money is a bit tight currently. I don't know why I lied about this, I guess I was worried the police would ask why I didn't go with her and that being suspicious. As expected, they say a police officer would be by to take a statement and start an investigation.

Two police officers come within the hour and I start my best distraught husband act. I give them some recent photos, pulling them from Sam's Instagram. I give them a description of her car, though really, it's in my name, but I don't mention this. They ask if they can have a look around. "No," I say, too quickly I realize. "I mean, I don't mind."

I follow them room to room as they make note of everything. I'm a bit troubled when one of them jots something in their notebook while they're in my bedroom. In the closet, one cop asks how much clothes she brought and I say that I don't know, probably enough for a week or so. They jot something else down. When they check out the bathroom, they find a pair of panties which Anna left and I had missed while cleaning. My face blushes, but I don't say anything, hoping they will assume it's Sam's. When they finish, they give me a card with a phone number to call if I hear anything from Sam. I thank them and shut the door, nearly collapsing in a shaky fluster. I need a drink.

23

Sam

Sunlight streaks through the bright orange and yellow leafy canopy. At first, I'm confused, forgetting where I am, even forgetting why I'm naked. Every part of me aches in seemingly unique ways. My feet are pins and needles and my leg muscles are sore. I stop there, not wanting to do another mental inventory of all my woes. I can do that when I get out of this mess. *If* I get out of this mess. My butt feels frozen to the ground, while the rest of me doesn't feel overly cold. I may have had more trouble sleeping in the cold had I not found the bushes to surround me and help insulate my body heat. I stretch my arms and arch my back, multiple joints popping and cracking loudly.

There's one thing I can help, which is my swollen, engorged breast. I gently squeeze on it, cupping underneath with my left hand while pressing down with my right palm. Breastmilk jettisons out, coating the bush as well as my tummy and thighs. I don't care, it just feels good to get the pressure out. I get sickened when the milk covering me reminds me of the old man and I stop. I've relieved enough pressure for now.

As I am about to stand, I hear movement nearby. Something or someone big is moving around near my hiding spot with heavy feet. The sunlight which breaks through the trees overhead is shining directly in my eyes, likely what woke me in the first place, also causing me to be unable to see who or what is walking around nearby. I forget that I have a large knife at my side when the large head pokes through the bush in front of me.

It's a big, black bear. Its nose twitches upward with each sniff as it smells the air around me. I'm frozen, unable to move, hoping that I'm convincingly playing dead. Its cold wet nose glides along my face. Its head is huge, bigger than I imagined a bear's head to be. Even if I'm quick and precise with the knife, it's very unlikely that I would be able to stop the bear before it mauls me. The best I can hope for is that if I remain completely still, it will leave me alone. The bear's head is as large as my torso. It sniffs further down to my chest to the large burn where my breast was removed. It gives a tentative lick at the burned area and I wince. My heart is pounding through my chest.

Its breath is a fog which smells like blood and earth. The bear's black-furred head continues moving down, sniffing loudly, a mist of mucus spraying with each sniff. Its muzzle finally rests between my legs which are still relaxed open from when I was sleeping. I tense when the bear's large mouth opens. I believe that the giant beast is about to bite me, maybe even use its mouth to drag me out in the open before tearing me to pieces.

Instead, its tongue laps out, running gently up from my asshole and between my lips. The bear's tongue is warm, soft and sticky, and not entirely unpleasant, but I'm afraid that the bear will harm me. The bear licks again, this time its tongue flicking inside of me for a second before drawing back into its mouth. I consider moving the bear's head gently aside but am immensely afraid that any action on my part would lead to swift and devastating violence, so I lie as still as possible, trembling, waiting for the bear to move on and leave me alone.

It licks again, even deeper than before. Soon, the bear's long pink tongue extends fully inside me, pushing, and twisting as it pulls back out and into the beast's mouth. I feel heat rise to my cheeks and can't believe that I'm becoming aroused from an animal. The bear issues a heavy, hot breath against my crotch and the inside of my thighs, then plunges its tongue back inside me forcefully as if it's drinking honey from a beehive as I've seen bears do in cartoons. I can feel additional heat growing from between my legs and rising up my spine. The bear pushes its tongue in me again, filling me, and it growls deeply, creating a vibration which echoes to the nerves in my clit, emanating through my pelvis, bringing me to the edge of orgasm. It plunges its tongue in deep again and emits a low, long growl, vibrating against my clit, pushing me over the edge. My legs shudder with the immense orgasm that I'm completely not ready for, finding myself unthinkingly stroking the top of the bear's head affectionately, petting it as it laps up my juices. The bear thrusts its tongue inside me one last time and I can feel it twist and flick around while it's in there, pressing roughly against the roof of my vagina, my G spot, before it draws out slowly and back into the bear's drooling wet mouth. It grunts then brings its head back up. It sniffs my face, then stares at me once more. I feel a deep connection to the bear, as if we are the same in some way, our souls linked. It then pulls its head out of the bush and pads heavily away, crunching leaves and sticks as it goes, disappearing into the forest.

The orgasm dulls a lot of the pain throughout my body. I feel flush with a new life and vigor, ready to tackle the day, optimistic that I will find someone who can help me. I stand and dust the crunched up dead leaves from my bare butt. I pull the knife up and return to the stream, keeping an eye out for the bear. Cool air blows off the thin water. I decide I should stay in the relative warmth of the woods after I get more water to drink ahead of my journey. The water is cool and refreshing as it was before, but now that I'm more hydrated it doesn't taste quite as amazing as it did last night.

In the daylight, I can see tiny silver minnows dancing around in the shallow water, almost swimming at the same pace of the water upstream so that they seem to be swimming in place. It reminds me of my tranquil moment at sea during my cruise. I feel a connection with nature, at peace for the first time in a long time.

If it weren't so cold, I would walk through the stream

itself to avoid walking barefoot on the hard stones lining the creek, but I know that my feet would likely freeze off should I attempt that. Instead, I return to the woods, keeping close to the creek and following it downstream. The leaves above and ahead are a watercolor of reds, yellows, oranges, greens, and browns, dotting the trees I can see in the distance. There seems to be no end to the forest in any direction, but particularly ahead, as the stream and downhill terrain descend into fog. I don't make it far downhill before I hear from the other side of the stream a shout, "Freeze, bitch!" It's the old man.

For once, I don't listen. I don't even look in his direction before I take off, running deeper into the woods on my side of the brook. I dash between trees and shrubs gracefully like a deer running from a wolf, as if I know these woods, as if I've lived here my entire life. A loud crack startles me—*lightning?*—and a tree near me explodes in splinters. It's a near miss. The old man is armed. Behind me, I hear heavy footsteps pounding through the stream toward me. Birds take flight from the noise, scattering. Squirrels and chipmunks also scatter, deftly wiggling their ways up trees as I pass. Sharp sticks stab my feet, but I ignore this. If I'm caught, I will be dragged back to that house and I'll never see the light of day again.

I hear the gun again and a second later I can hear a round whiz by me, ripping through nearby leaves. *Fffft!* The heavy pounding footsteps are gaining on me despite how fast I am running and how much I dodge around the thicks trees. It must be the big man that visited me the previous night, the *murderer* who killed Emma. I look for cover to hide in though I know the big man must be close enough that hiding somewhere wouldn't fool him anyway. That's when I see the brambles, tightly woven vines that I believe I can dive under, if I can just reach them in time. I would be like Br'er Rabbit, hiding from the farmer.

But before I get there, the big man tackles me like a football player, knocking the wind out of me as he slams me to the ground in a scratchy slide on my belly. The sudden weight on my still-engorged breast is excruciating. It feels like it's about to burst. I blearily try to stand, my arms and legs slipping in the dead leaves. The big man grabs my ankles and pulls me to him. He climbs on top of me and sits on my back with his enormous weight. I can't breathe from him compressing my lungs. I try to huff in air desperately. I can't move. I sob in defeat.

A moment later, the old man crunches up behind us, out of breath. "Nice job, Big Joe. You did real good. Makes up for lettin' her get out." So, the big man must have admitted to his part in my escape. He had only left the door unlocked, but that was enough for me to get the knife at least. *The knife!* I try to bring my hand around to stab the man in the leg to get him off of me, but he grabs my wrist in his meaty hand and squeezes hard. I can hear the joint crunching beneath his grip so I release the cleaver, letting it drop to the dirt. The old man walks around, his gun pointed at me as if I can really do anything to get up, then he picks up the knife. "This is *my* knife!" he says, tucking the blade into his coat pocket. "You stole *my* knife, you bitch."

"No shit," I sputter blood from a busted lip I gained from the fall. The big man presses his knee into my back even harder.

The old man tuts. "Yer gonna think about what you did, runnin' off like that, and stealin' my property. Yer gonna get most o' yer punishment when we get home, after I fix the bed. But fer now, yer gonna learn who ya belong to. And then yer gonna be a good girl and not try to run off again. Else I'm gonna have Big Joe here knock yer head on the rocks a coupla times to get you to sleep. Now I don't wanna risk killin' ya if I don't have to but I will if needs must." He shoulders his rifle, then says, "Alright, Big Joe, go on spread 'er legs fer me. And stay on 'er back, mind. Don't want the bitch scurryin' off again." The big man puts more weight on his knees and less on my back, letting me take in a sharp breath. He holds me down with his large hands while he pivots around, then seats himself on my upper back. I feel a rib crack beneath his weight and scream into the dirt. He leans forward toward my ass and grabs my thighs, then spreads them apart. I strain to keep my legs together but am no match for the big man. He's too strong. I hear the old man set his rifle on the ground, then unzip his pants.

Just as the old man approaches me and I wince in anticipation of him entering me forcibly, something crashes through the brush to my right and sends Big Joe sprawling. I twist around in surprise to see that it's the bear! The large black bear is on top of Big Joe, who is screaming incoherently in alarm. The old man, whose hardened red and gray dick is jutting out of his open fly, fully displaying his angry infections, bends down to pick the rifle up and cocks it as he stands. The bear makes a mighty swipe at Big Joe's head, rocking it roughly to the side. To anyone else, this may have been a deadly blow, but the large man is unphased, still trying to fight the bear off of him. The old man is not at the right angle to take down the bear and can only shoot it in its hind legs. Blood and fur pop outward from the wound.

The bear jumps off of Big Joe with a grunt and turns to face the old man. He readies his rifle, pointing it at the bear's face and I kick him as hard as I can in the back of the knee, sending the old man's shot wild, his rifle pointing up. More birds scatter. The bear bites at the man's belly, ripping away clothes and flesh. His intestines neatly stay put for a second before unspooling and falling to the ground with a wet slopping sound, like canned spaghetti. The old man attempts to aim his rifle at the bear again, but is having a hard time maintaining a steady hand. Big Joe leaps onto the bear's back and wraps his wide arms around its neck. He locks his hands together, trying to choke the bear.

The bear lunges forward and grabs a length of intestines, then begins pulling at the old man's guts like it's playing tug of war. The old man fires off another round, which blasts through Big Joe's forehead, spraying blood and brain onto his and the bear's backs. Big Joe is dead, but his body maintains its grip around the bear's neck. The bear releases the old man's guts and pounds into him, its giant paws landing hard on his shoulders and neck, causing him to crumple to the ground. The bear has much of its weight on top of him now so he can't raise his rifle. The beast snaps its jaws at the old man's face, which the man blocks with his arm. I can hear the old man's arm bones crunch under mighty jaws. The bear bites again at his face, finds purchase on the flesh of his cheeks and nose, and rips his face free from his skull. He screams in pain. I can't believe the old man is still alive. One of his eyes is dangling, bouncing around the side of his shredded face, seeming to look from me to the forest floor in a pendulum sway.

The bear bites again at his face, pulling away muscle and crunching his cheek and jaw bones into splinters. He screams again, still alive. "Get the fuck off me you goddamn bitch!" he says. His arms and legs flail but with the bear's front paws weighing on his chest, along with Big Joe's added weight on the bear's back, he can't do much more. The bear brings its jaws closed on the old man's throat and rips away the soft pale flesh, blood spraying everywhere. The old man gargles, choking on blood, still flailing weakly against the bear's front legs. The bear lifts a few inches off the old man then brings its full weight back down. I can hear the old man's ribs shattering beneath the weight. With this, the old man stops moving, aside from a few errant spasms.

The bear drags the old man by his destroyed head, back through the bushes, leaving his rifle in the dirt. Big Joe slides off the side of the bear as it walks away. I see for the first time as the bear departs that it's pregnant.

I shoulder the rifle, then consider following the bear so that I can take what I need from the old man's corpse. Maybe get a look at the bear eating him. I remember he was wearing a backpack, possibly with supplies or some sort of communication device, plus the knife is in his jacket pocket, but I decide not to risk it. Though the bear was gentle with me this morning and didn't make any moves to attack me just now, I don't know what she would do if I were to try to approach her den.

Instead, I find Big Joe's body not far from where the confrontation occurred. When he fell off the bear, he landed on his back, so his face is on full display. His entire forehead seems to be gone, replaced with a gaping hole. Inside, I can see that his brain is a bloody mush. Despite having seen comparably terrible things done to me, I can't help but vomit at the sight, spewing mostly stream water and bile onto the forest floor.

Once I regain my composure, I check his pockets, finding only lint, a random assortment of coins, small toys, and pebbles, and a partially eaten sandwich. I'm hungry, but don't trust whatever sort of meat would be in the sandwich, so I leave it all with the body. With a grunt, I lift the heavy corpse onto its side, then undo the blue jeans and pull them down to the big man's ankles. I remove each of the boots and jeans, leaving him the blood-soaked t-shirt. I can't help but notice that the briefs he's wearing are shit-stained. I bring the jeans and boots back to where I was, away from the corpse, then put them on. I'm almost swimming in the jeans, but am able to keep them around my waist by pulling the belt as tight as I can get it, then tucking it twice around itself. I roll up the legs of the pants and tuck them into the boots. I realize I probably look silly, wearing a blue jean version of harem pants and too-large boots, while being topless, but I appreciate the added warmth and protection that the clothing provides.

With the bear dragging the old man away, I lost the knife, but I now have a presumably-loaded rifle, which should be enough of a defense should coyotes find me at night, or if the bear changes her mind about not seeing me as a threat or food. I head back to the stream and look as far as I can. I could continue following it down in the hopes that it leads somewhere, but I don't see anywhere it would lead, so I would have to walk for a very long time before finding someone, if I ever do. Considering I don't know what vegetation is safe to eat, nor do I know how to hunt, I would likely starve to death before reaching any assistance. My only other path is to try to return to the house.

OSCAR BRADY

With the old man and big guy gone, the house doesn't seem so scary. And now that I'm armed, I could take on the woman. But I'm not sure how I got here, having walked most of the way at night, not that I would recognize one tree from another should I have taken the route by day. I look around in desperate confusion, my hunger not making the decision any easier, when I spot something very promising on the ground. In the grass and mud beyond the rocks of the stream are a set of deep boot-prints, matching the very boots I'm wearing. I grin at my luck and follow the boots into the forest, back toward the house I escaped.

24

Daniel

Sometime later, I'm conscious and looking around blearily. I wonder briefly if everything I remember happening before I blacked out was just a dream, or a nightmare really, but a short look at my bloody, mangled crotch puts that notion to rest. My crotch is still oozing thick blood, albeit slowly. I feel nauseous and angry, but for the first time in a long time, not suicidal in the slightest.

"Oh Danny Boy, the pipes, the pipes are calling..." I swear I can really hear Ben singing this as he's done countless times in the past, this time reverberating in the mostly empty dungeon, but I know that it can't be true. I grip the pipe joint and twist with all my might. The metal groans as I loosen it. Now that it's loosened, I'm able to untwist it more easily. My hands burn, but I ignore this. I ignore all of the pain. I keep twisting the pipe joint, feeling a cool liquid coming out. Judging by the smell, it's not water. Soon, the joint comes off the pipe and I'm able to pull the pipe below free from it. I quickly pull my roped wrists through the gap.

I try to stand, but quickly fall back on my ass. I'm able to get up on the second try, woozily, then look around the room. There isn't much to it. There's the door, which may or may not be locked. There's Ben, dead and still tied to the wall. *Wish you were here.* And there's the pile of boxes, some saying they contain lye and some marked "Bunny Pelts." That's when it clicks for me, I remember what "bunny" means. The girl had called me and Ben bunnies. That's what they call the people they capture.

I stagger over to the box, then remember that my arms are tied behind my back. I foolishly try to bring my arms over my head which doesn't work. I sit back down on the cold concrete floor and wiggle my bound wrists under my butt, then past my thighs. I have a bit more trouble getting past the length of my legs, stretching my sore muscles as much as I can. One foot at a time, I'm able to push my legs through the loop created by my arms and the rope. I'm still bound but at least my hands are in front of me now.

I feel a hard cramp double me over. I then remember the corn that crazy woman stuffed up my ass like a Thanksgiving turkey. I'm not going to be able to shit again until I get surgery, I just know it. But fuck it, I know now that I want to live. Even though my dick was just chewed off – that thing got me into more trouble than it was worth. I'll even do the stupid chemo or whatever the doctors suggest.

I go to the top box marked "Bunny Pelts" with black marker and bring it down to the floor. I unfold the top flaps of the box and immediately recognize my duffel. As expected, the phrase marked on these boxes refers to the belongings the family steals from their captives. I open the duffel and pull out a slightly dirty pair of jeans. With a bit of effort, I'm able to pull them over my legs and hips. It probably isn't doing anything to slow or stop the bleeding, but at least it's something. I reach in the bag again and find what I'm looking for after digging through my dirty clothes.

A little deeper in the box, I discover what looks to be a diaper bag. I paw around inside and find another thing I was looking for—a phone. The iPhone is still powered on and, based on the battery icon, it won't be for much longer. I'm unable to get past the lock screen, but find a link that says "Emergency" and press it. It gives me the opportunity to dial 911, which I do even though the icon at the top of the screen indicates that the phone doesn't have any reception, either because of the remote location I'm at, the fact that I'm in a basement, or a combination of the two. Somehow, miraculously, the call goes through.

The operator says, "This is 9-1-1, what is your location and the nature of your emergency?"

I speak softly. "Hello, I don't know where I'm at. I'm in a house somewhere in the middle of nowhere most likely. These people, they—"

"Hello? If you're speaking, I can't hear you."

"Fuck," I say, and bring the phone with me as I make my way to the basement door. I can hear the emergency services operator speaking, though her voice is broken up.

I put the phone in my jeans pocket, leaving the call connected, while I try the doorknob, which is apparently unlocked. I open it slowly, wanting to be as silent as possible. I creep up the stairs, creaking with every step. Upstairs, I hear a television playing what sounds like a commercial. I don't know which one of the three maniacs I will encounter first, if there's only three of them, but I know this is my only way out of this place.

At the top of the stairs is another door, also closed. I slowly, carefully, turn the knob and push the door gently open. The noise from the television amplifies while I open the door. I find myself in a kitchen which smells of cooked meat. Considering what this family seems to dine on, I don't want to know what—or *who*—the meat came from. *Ben.* Around the corner from the door, I can hear the TV, understanding that this must be the living room. I step softly into the room to find the girl, Krystal, sitting on the floor cross-legged only a few feet away from the TV, her eyes fixed raptly on the screen. Her face and bare chest are still coated in my blood, which has dried. She's mindlessly rubbing her tummy as if she can already feel the baby moving around, if she's even pregnant to begin with.

"Hands above your head," I say, pointing my revolver at the woman. It's only now, while I'm standing here with a gun pointed at one of the family members, that I remember that the gun is empty. At no point during the road trip did I have the opportunity to purchase ammunition. So, I have to bluff.

Krystal doesn't move her hands and stays seated. "How the fuck did *you* get out?"

"Not important. I said put your hands above your head."

Krystal rolls her eyes and slowly puts her hands above her head, smirking like this is a game. My blood covers her palms and most of her arms. When she raises her arms, her blood-soaked tits lift, creating parentheses of clean flesh beneath her small breasts. Blood is even in her armpit hair. She catches me glancing at her breasts and grins. "Even without their junk, all men are perverts. Not that I can talk."

"Where are the others?"

Krystal looks around, still smirking. "Other *whats*? You'll have to be more specific, bunny boy. And whatever you are gettin' at, can you make it fast? The commercials are almost done and I don't wanna miss nothin'."

"The old man and the other... man. Where are they?"

"Oh, they're around." The woman glances back at the TV, bored. She yawns, then drops her arms back to the floor.

"Keep them up," I say. Now that I've remembered the gun isn't loaded, my plan has changed from revenge to escape. I just need to get the woman to tell me where the keys to the pickup are so I can get out of here.

"You know what I think?" Krystal calmly gets off the floor. I wave the gun in an attempt to intimidate her, but it doesn't work. "I think that if *I* was a stupid ol' boy bunny who just got his pecker bit off, and *I* figured out some way out of *my* rope and got *my* hands on a gun somehow—miracle after miracle, I swear —that I would want one of two things." Krystal stands akimbo but with two fingers raised. "Suicide or revenge." She crosses her arms, grinning away at me. I have no words. "Now, suicide

I definitely get. What fun is life if you can't fuck no more? I didya like a praying mantis, didn't I?" She pauses to laugh at her own joke. "But obviously, that's not what you went with since you came all the way up here. So, what's left?" I'm getting nervous, knowing where this is going. "Sweet revenge! You got every right to be mad at me! I just ate your big ol' meaty cock—and it was mighty big I tell ya, but that's okay 'cause I'm eatin' for two—so you got a damn good reason to want me dead! And my Grandaddy and Big Joe, he's my brother by the way, they done took your boyfriend's feet off. Where's he at, anyway? Why didn't you let him loose while you were at it?"

"He's dead, you cunt."

"Ah, yeah, that makes sense. We got a little overzealous if you know what I mean. Normally we don't take so much off so fast. Just a little at a time. Cut it, cauterize it, cook it. Keeps the meat fresh that way, much better than the fridge and *miles* better than frozen bunny. Blegh!" She sticks a finger in her mouth and pokes out her tongue as if to illustrate her point. "Real shame he's dead now. Guess we gotta throw him in the freezer pretty soon before he starts to go bad."

"Listen, I—"

"Where was I? Oh yeah, revenge. If you was after revenge, you woulda shot me by now. So, I think—" The commercials end and the program comes back on. It's a soap opera. "Oh, shit, it's back on. Shh!"

I'm confused. I thought I would have the power in the situation, but she doesn't seem to care that I have a gun. She's called my bluff, but I have to keep it up anyway if I want out of this hell. "Look, I'm no killer. But I will if I have to—"

"Shut up! I can't hear what they're sayin'!" She uses a clunky remote to turn up the volume.

"Hey!" I wave the revolver at her again. "Give me the keys to the truck or I will shoot you!"

"Arghhh!" The woman huffs and slaps her legs in exasperation. "Your gun ain't got no bullets in it!" She looks at me, studying my reaction. "Well go on then, prove me wrong! Shoot me, or shut up and let me watch my soaps!"

I charge forward, swinging the butt of the revolver at her temple, but she easily dodges my sluggish movements. The phone falls out of my pocket and hits the floor, then chimes its power down sound. I trip over the wooden coffee table and spill face first into the sofa. Krystal gets up and kicks me in the crotch. Though I have nothing there left for her to kick, the wound is fresh and the kick is excruciating. I scream in pain.

The woman laughs and says, "Oh, I completely forgot you ain't got balls to kick anymore!" I struggle to get back to my feet and Krystal kicks me back down. "Oh well, I guess I'll have to catch the rerun." She turns the TV off, then says, "Don't want no spoilers, though!" I'm able to roll off the couch and am on my back, still wincing in pain. I start to sit up. "Oh, where you goin', bunny boy?" She kicks me against the side of my head, knocking me onto my back again. She presses her bare foot onto my crotch, hard. Black spots cloud the edges of my vision and I nearly faint.

I realize I'm still holding the gun, raise it to point it at Krystal's face and pull the trigger. It clicks loudly and Krystal flinches. Apparently, she, too, was bluffing, but I have no way to prove her wrong. Her flinch and disorientation gives me time to scramble to my feet, albeit dizzily. "Just give me the keys and I'll be out of here," I say, hoping to sound more confident than I feel.

She laughs. "You mighta startled me with the dry fire, call it force of habit. But that gun ain't loaded." I pull the hammer back. "But Grandaddy did teach me to treat all guns like they was loaded, so let's play along for now." She puts her hands up. "Say I can't get the keys for ya 'cause Grandaddy has 'em on 'im. What then?"

I think on it for a second, then wave her to the couch. "Sit down. We'll just wait 'til he comes back." She sits on the couch, spreading her legs. *Not very ladylike,* I think. She smiles up at me again, noticing me looking between her legs, and shakes her head as if tutting at me.

"Sounds boring. Can I at least put the TV back on?"

"No."

"Ugh, you suck." She crosses her arms and puts her lower lip out in an exaggerated pout. "Your gun probably ain't loaded. You're lucky I'm pregnant and don't wanna risk the baby gettin' hurt. But when Grandaddy and Big Joe come back, they'll make short work of you."

I find a chair and sit across the room from Krystal. "Yeah, we'll see."

We wait for what feels like hours. I almost consider Krystal's request to turn the television on. Just when I had given up on the old man returning, I hear footsteps approaching behind me. I make sure the gun remains pointed at Krystal.

But instead of the old man's voice, I hear a woman's voice. "Who the fuck are you?" I turn and see a topless woman pointing a rifle into the room. *Is this another member of this fucked up family?* One of her breasts is missing and in its place is deeply burned flesh, covered in blisters. She's wearing very baggy jeans with a belt holding them up and cartoonishly large boots. She either has been in the house the whole time or must have entered through a back door because I would have heard her come in through the front.

Krystal gasps and says, "The girl bunny!"

The woman points the rifle at Krystal and says, "Well, there you are. I've been looking forward to our reunion." Considering I'm dressed fairly similarly to the new arrival and she looks as though she's been tortured, with her missing breast and one hand missing all of its fingers, she must be another victim of the family. Not to mention that Krystal just called her a bunny.

"They were keeping me in the basement," I offer as a way of introduction. "Killed my friend. And this bitch ate parts of me right off my body." I gesture at Krystal with the revolver.

"Oh, don't be coy, bunny boy." She looks at the woman with the rifle. "I ate his dick and balls." She looks back to me. "Damn tasty too! Wish I could have seconds!"

"Shut the fuck up!" The woman says, firing a round into the couch near the woman. Couch fluff flies out and the bullet hole smokes. Krystal startles but doesn't scream. She speaks more calmly to me. "They kept me here too, tortured me. Killed my baby."

"Oh my God..." I say. "That's awful."

"And now this bitch is going to die." The woman cocks the rifle and aims it at Krystal again. "Any last words?"

Someone pounds at the door, causing all three of us to startle. "Police, open up!"

I shout, "It's the old man, he's lying!"

The woman with the rifle smiles and says, "Nope, can't be. The rest of this bitch's family are dead."

"Noooo!" Krystal screams and runs at the woman with the rifle.

The door is kicked in and a police officer enters with his gun drawn. "Drop the weapon!" he shouts. "Hands in the air!" Krystal halts mid-charge. The woman was just about to shoot Krystal when the police entered. She looks like she nearly does anyway, but thinks better of it and halts.

The seat I'm in is around the corner from the entry, so I'm not sure if the cop even sees me, but I stand with my hands raised anyway, leaving the revolver on the chair. The jumpy cop, not ready for a black man moving in his peripheral quickly shoots three rounds at what he perceives to be a threat.

I crumple to the ground. The woman with the rifle slowly raises her hands, letting the rifle drop to her side, only held by its strap.

"Thank God you're here!" Krystal says, pointing at the woman. "Get that bitch too! She kilt my family!"

She's lying, I want to say, but can't speak. I feel a warmth blossoming from the center of my back where the cop shot me. I don't see an exit wound on my chest. I can't breathe. The cop must have shot me in a lung. Everything goes black. I hear Ben one last time. *Wish you were here.*

25

Sam

Two police officers enter the house to find me pointing a rifle at Krystal. Before I can do anything in reaction, they shoot the man who claimed to be another one of the family's victims. There's a revolver on the arm of the chair where the man was seated, but he wasn't touching it when he was shot. I hope he's alright, not just because as far as I can tell he's an innocent man, but also because he would be able to corroborate my story. I can't see how bad the shot is, and am too scared of being shot as well to venture a look. I put my hands up and the police handcuff me after removing the rifle, reciting my Miranda rights.

Krystal shouts her story to the officers before I can say anything. She claims that I had burst in with the rifle and told her that I'd killed her family and was about to kill her. Technically all of this is true, but the woman is excluding some very important details to the story.

"They kidnapped me." I'm sobbing and can't say much more. The police pat down my legs, feeling for any other weapons in the jeans I stole from the big man, then drape a blanket over my shoulders and escort me out to the police car. I wonder how the police knew to come. The man must have called them, the one with the revolver. One of the officers sits in the front seat to radio in a status while the other returns to the house. Then he leaves me alone in the car with the engine running. They must be questioning Krystal, getting her side of the story first. *There's no way they can believe her*, I think. *If they search the house, who knows what they'll find.* The wait feels interminable. Another squad car arrives with its lights on and two more officers exit the vehicle. Neither seem to notice me in the back of this car.

I actually feel safe for the first time. Though I'm worried I'll be in some sort of trouble from this, falsely accused by the crazy woman, at least I'll be relatively safe compared to my life for the past several days. This feeling of security coupled with the heat blasting through the car causes me to doze. I wake to the front car doors opening and closing, the two officers returning to their vehicle. "Where are you taking me?" I ask, quietly. I almost repeat myself when one responds.

"There's an ambulance on the way that will take you to the hospital. We've got a lot of questions so we'll be following you there."

"You didn't believe her, did you? She's fucking crazy. She and her family are lunatics. They're cannibals."

"Calm down, ma'am. No, we didn't believe her," the cop in the driver's seat says. He looks to his partner. "Cannibals? Jesus..."

The ambulance arrives and the police help me out of the car. The paramedics assist me into the back of the ambulance, which I'm surprised that they don't use a gurney, not that I need one. They first check the wounds on my right breast and hand, then the cut on my foot and all the other minor wounds throughout my body. As they tend to these wounds, one asks, "Holy shit, what happened?"

"A lot," I say.

"Yeah, no kidding."

They tell me that my wounds are mostly healed, though I have an infection on my hand where my fingers were removed. I'm also severely dehydrated, so they run an IV. Otherwise, my vitals are good. At the hospital, the police visit my room while

I wait for the doctor to see me. They don't advise me again of my right to remain silent or to seek an attorney, leading me to believe they don't think I'm guilty of anything. They ask me for my name and when I give it, they eye each other then look back at me. "Your family's been looking for you. The Virginia State Police put out a nationwide bulletin that you went missing somewhere between Virginia and Missouri. I'm sure they'll be happy to hear you're alright. Well, mostly alright." *Virginia State Police,* I think. *So that means Jared was looking for me after all.*

They then ask me what happened and I cover everything I can remember, starting with how I ran over what looked to be deer bones and how the old man picked me up. I recount everything, stopping to cry when I get to Emma's murder, including all the methods of torture inflicted upon me, how I escaped, the bear attacking the two men, and how I got back to the house and snuck in through the back door. The police take copious notes, asking for additional details on where I believe my car was left. They seem incredulous when I describe the bear attack, wondering why the bear would attack the men and leave me alone. I, of course, leave out the part of how the bear woke me up.

When the doctor enters, the police leave, giving me and the doctor each a business card, and tell me that a detective may be by later to ask more questions. The doctor performs many of the same tests as the paramedics and prescribes me some antibiotics, ointments, and heavy painkillers. My wounds are all closed so I won't need surgery, at least not right away, though the doctor mentions I would be a candidate for autologous breast reconstruction and a prosthetic for my hand. When I say I wouldn't be able to afford that, the doctor says that most likely the people who did these things to me would foot the bill. And if they can't afford it, the state would cover it by their prison sentence. I can't see them having a bunch of money lying around, but don't push the issue. I'm then admitted into a quiet room with a bed to rest in and for monitoring.

When I wake the next morning, my mother is there, watching the TV in my room. When she sees that I'm awake, she dramatically gets up and hugs me, crying. "Oh, my goodness! First my stroke, and then you and Emma go missing. I swear bad things always happen to me in threes!" I almost laugh scoffingly. It's pretty typical of my mom to make this about her.

"I'm okay, Mom. Just a little beat up." I don't want to talk about Emma, not yet.

"A *little beat up?!* Your breast is missing and you don't have any fingers on your right hand! What on Earth happened to you?! And where's my grandbaby? The doctors and police won't tell me anything!"

"There were some bad people," I say. "They hurt me and Emma, but I was able to get away." I leave it at that. "Sorry, I don't feel much like talking right now. I'm so tired."

"Well, I'm just glad you're alright. I got so worried when you said you were coming to see me and you never showed. Then you didn't answer your phone, so I thought you must be mad at me for some reason or another, you're always up in your feelings about something, but then your husband said he didn't know where you were at either! You know, I told you that you shouldn't be driving around alone, especially with the baby—"

I cut her off there. "No, this is not my fault. Contrary to what you seem to believe, not everything is my fault and you, *mother*, do not always know best. This horrible, awful thing that happened to me is not my fault—it's nobody's fault except the people who did it to me. And for God's sake, I lost my *child*. That happened to *me*. Stop making everything about you, because we're all sick of it."

"Well, clearly you're tired and need to rest," she says and packs her purse. "Call me when you're in a better mood."

"Yeah, we'll see," I say. In a huff, she promptly leaves.

That afternoon, Jared visits. I wake from another nap to

157

see him with his phone to his ear, probably taking a work call. When he sees that I'm awake, he tells whoever he's talking to that he has to go. *That might be the first time he's wanted to talk to me over taking a work call,* I think.

"Oh, sweetie," Jared says, "the police told me that our baby's gone. I'm so sorry." My face scrunches as I break down. I haven't cried this hard since I first learned Emma had been murdered by the giant. It felt good seeing him shot, and standing over his dead body, but I know that his death will not bring Emma back. I don't think I would ever be able to have another child. They would just remind me too much of Emma. Jared reaches across the bed and hugs me. "Listen, the doctor says you can go home now if you're ready. No rush or anything. Each night you stay here is probably a thousand bucks, but we'll make it work. You take the time you need."

I'm shaken by the sudden change of topic, though I am eager to go home. "I'm ready," I say. "We can go home now." I start to get up, then Jared stops me and says that they said they wanted to wheel me out because of the painkillers I'm on. Jared walks out and flags a nurse to let them know I'm ready. A nurse comes in shortly after to give some aftercare recommendations, which Jared seems to only half pay attention to, saying "uh-huh," and "ok, got it" to move things along. I'm still a bit too woozy to remember much of what she says, but am okay with this when she mentions everything is in a printed packet. They help me downstairs while Jared pulls his car around.

The painkillers don't numb me enough to stop the panic attack I get while we're driving through the Appalachian Mountains. All I can think of is us hitting more deer bones and everything starting over, as if the old man isn't already dead, along with his murderous grandson. Jared obediently pulls over and helps me control my breathing. I refuse to leave the car until we get home though.

When we do, Jared helps me into the house and I collapse

on the bed, which has fresh sheets. Despite my grogginess, I'm surprised at the sheets being clean. Jared *never* washes the sheets or comforter and would always get irritated with me if I delayed him going to bed so that I could change the sheets in the evening, having forgotten to do it while taking care of Emma.

The next day, I wander into Emma's room and sit on the floor, taking in the smell and the sight of her room which has gone untouched since I left with her a million years ago. I almost feel like I can see Emma sleeping in the crib, but it's just a wishful illusion. Jared, holding a cup of coffee, finds me in Emma's room. "I can get everything out of here and repaint if you want," he says, likely trying to be consoling.

"No, please don't." I sniffle. "I need this room the way it is."

"That's fine, too." Jared looks around the room quietly for a moment, then says, "Hey, I made coffee and breakfast. You should eat."

I sigh. "I'll be in there in a minute. I just want to sit here for a little while. I can still smell her in here."

"Okay," Jared says. "Well, if you need anything, I'll be in the kitchen. I took the day off to stay home with you. I really shouldn't be taking leave right now, but I know you need support right now. I love you."

"I love you, too," I say, still looking at Emma's crib. Jared leaves me to my grief.

I don't know how much longer I can go on like this. I've only been home for a day, but I know I will never get over what I went through, nor losing Emma. It still feels like only minutes since I was in that house. Everything's moved so quickly since then. I don't want to try to forget Emma as Jared suggested by saying he could take all of Emma's stuff out and repaint the room. She had filled a part of me that had always been missing and I had just not known it. Feeling her plump, warm body nestled to my chest was heaven. I try to remember the feeling, but come up short. Instead, I feel an icy emptiness where my breast should be. The doctor had mentioned breast reconstruction surgery, and Jared had brought it up a few times on the car ride home as well. He says he just wants me to be able to go back to normal, as normal as I can. Jared said it was the only way I would be able heal.

I put my hand where my breast once hung. I was given ointment to put on the burns, which I've done for myself. I was afraid Jared might not do it gently enough. He also seems to be disgusted by my new body. I try to remember the way Emma looked feeding from my breast, but remembering Emma only brings me back to the sound of the thud, Emma's death, and the sandwich. Thanks to that family, I can't think of my baby without remembering how her flesh had tasted. I feel nauseous from the memory and leave Emma's room, not wanting to taint it further.

Jared is on the phone when I enter the kitchen, and strangely he blushes before he ends the call. "Who was that?" I ask.

"Oh, no one, I mean, someone from work. They really can't do anything without me there, apparently. Don't worry about it, though, I'll stay here with you." He runs over to the coffee pot and makes me a cup, then sets it on the table where a plate of food is waiting for me. "Oof, your chest looks awful," he says as I sit down. I'm wearing my robe so it must have opened when I sat for him to see.

"Yeah? No shit," I say.

"Alright, there's no reason to be rude. You know I miss, umm, our baby as much as you. We're both going through a lot here, so cut me some slack."

I stare off for a moment, then realize he'd forgotten her name again. "What's her name, Jared? What's our baby's name?"

Jared is silent, face turning red. "Why do you always have

160

to make everything into an argument? Just because I said 'our baby' doesn't mean I don't know her name."

"Then what's her name, Jared?" I push the food away in exasperation. "Tell me. You always would forget it and I'd have to remind you."

Jared steps away from the table looking flustered. Then he turns, face clearly showing he just remembered. "It was Emma! Our baby's name was Emma. See?"

I start crying at his use of the past tense. He so easily reconciles her death. As I'm looking down, I notice a long, red hair on my robe. My hair is mousey brown, and Jared's is short, black, and graying. Emma's sparse hair is—*was*—blonde. Jared seems to be heading out the door, grabbing his keys, when I ask, "Whose is this?" I hold out the red hair.

He freezes in his tracks, his face blanching. After a moment, he regains his composure and without looking at me says, "I don't know. It's your robe, isn't it?" He puts on his jacket. "I'm going for a drive. Letting off steam. Let you calm down too. Bye." And he's gone.

26

Jared

I've only had the wife back home for a day, or less really, and she's already being a Grade A Bitch. I've been treating her like a princess since I drove all the way to some hospital in West Virginia to get her, and still, she's more controlling than ever. I need to see Anna, let off some steam. I actually haven't seen her since kicking her out the day I called the cops. I didn't want them randomly stopping by to ask questions and seeing Anna there. That would be very bad.

I try giving Anna another call since I had to hang up on her when Sam walked in the kitchen. I'm going to have her meet me at the motel, our spot, so we can fool around for an hour or two. She doesn't pick up, which is strange, so I get to the motel and book the room, then try again. Finally, she answers.

"Hi," she says. She sounds a bit flustered.

"Hey, babe, good news – I don't have to worry about the cops sniffing around anymore, so we're in the clear. What do you say we meet at the mo—"

"Listen, we can't see each other anymore." She lets out a long breath. "I told Mark about the affair."

"You *what?*" I stand from the motel bed where I was seated and begin pacing the room.

"I told him everything. I don't know, I just felt bad. He really is a sweet guy and I've been doing him dirty, and that's not me. I mean, that's not who I want to be."

"What are you saying, Anna? Why would you tell Mark?

That ruins everything!"

"I know, and I don't care. Look, Jared, he's willing to give me another chance. But I can't see you anymore, like, ever. I'm quitting my job in the morning."

I pull at my hair. "You've gotta be fucking kidding me!" I scream into the phone. I pound a fist on the wall.

"Goodbye, Jared," she says and hangs up.

I throw my phone at the bed and pace the room some more, pissed. I rip open the bourbon I'd brought in for Anna and I to share. I pour a finger into the plastic motel cup and it goes down with a burn. So, I decide it would be better with ice. I'll have a few drinks, then go back home and see if Sam is ready to apologize. If not, then I don't know what I'll do.

I grab the plastic bucket from the room and carry it to the ice machine, which is where I see a blonde bimbo at the Coke vending machine. She's young looking, at most 22, and wearing a cropped t-shirt and pink sweatpants. Her nipples are hard points in the cold November weather.

"Got a dollar?" she says, biting her lip.

27

Krystal

Those cops arrest me even though I was tellin' the truth about the girl bunny killin' Grandaddy and Big Joe. She said so herself! I suppose it woulda went better had I thought to take a shower before startin' to watch my soaps. Get the boy bunny's blood off me. But how was I to know that the boy bunny would also get out and somehow call the cops? I guess I should be thankful the boy bunny called the cops because otherwise the girl bunny mighta shot me like she did to Grandaddy and Big Joe.

Real shame about the boy bunny though. The cops don't even check on him after shootin' him. Who knows, he coulda still been alive? So, they end up handcuffin' me and takin' me to the jail where they make me take a cold shower and put on a cute gray outfit with a number on the shirt. Before the shower, they use a swab to get some of the blood off me which I know won't be good for me if they figure out whose blood that is. They swab a few different areas prob'ly thinkin' it might be a buncha different blood, but I coulda told 'em it's all from the boy bunny that they shot. It also won't look good if they start pokin' around the house, but I suppose they can't do that without a warrant. I know that's only a matter of time though so I gotta get outta here and hide out somewhere before they figure things out.

I'm the only one here in the jail part so it's pretty quiet. Pretty boring too, since there's just the cot, a little sink, and a commode. Before long, this cute, ugly middle-aged policeman comes by to check on me. "Hey," I say to him. "Don't I get a phone call?"

"Don't believe everything you see in the movies," he says, pullin' at his belt.

"I'll suck your dick if you let me make a phone call. Gotta let me make it in private, though."

"You know they monitor all the calls coming out of here," he says. "Ain't no such thing as private."

"Maybe they do. I'll suck your dick right now anyway if you take me to the phones and let me make my phone call."

And I'm grinnin' 'cause he looks left and right as if to make sure ain't no one comin' and he pulls his little pecker out and puts it up against the cage. I bet he came down here just see if I'm a dirty little slut. So, I get down and pull as much of his dick as I can through the bars, which ain't much, and start suckin' on it. He gets hard but his pecker don't get no bigger really. It takes maybe thirty seconds of suckin' on the head of his dick 'cause that's all he can get through the bars before he's cummin' in my mouth and I drink it like a good girl. And it was a lot of cum! He must notta made cum in a while!

"Goddamn you're good," he says, puttin' his pecker away and zippin' up his cop pants. "I'll get the key. Be right back."

The key turns out to be a plastic card, which he swipes at the wall near the jailcell and then he opens the door. He puts me back in cuffs and takes me over to the hallway with the phones, which look like payphones from the movies but they don't take money. He stands there for a minute until I remind him that I said I want some privacy and he leaves me be. While he's walkin' away, I make my phone call which I don't really need privacy for. In fact, I don't need to even talk. It's a phone number Grandaddy had me memorize just in case this kinda thing happened. He done learnt from watchin' the terrorist wars on the news, about how the terrorists would set up bombs connected to phones and when you call 'em, they make the bomb go boom. I looked up how to do it on the Internet with my smart phone. It really is amazing what they got on there! Everything! All I can hope is that it works and our house just blew sky high. Ain't no way I can go back there anyway.

The reason I want privacy is because I need to get outta here! I was hopin' he wouldn't put me in cuffs, I mean I did just drink his cum. Whatever happened to chivalry? But beggars can't be choosers, I guess. I leave the phone danglin so he don't hear me hang it up and run off down the hallway in the opposite direction as where he went. I see the red signs on the ceiling that say "EXIT" and I follow those until I get to the emergency exit door. I know this will trigger some sort of alarm, but as long as I move fast, I can be outta here before they can get me.

I push the door open and run out as fast as my little legs will take me. Sure enough, an alarm starts goin' off. The jail is in the same building as the police station, so it ain't like there's guard towers or tall fences like you might see at a real prison. A real prison is where I mighta ended up had I not run, especially if that bomb didn't work and they find all the bunny meat we got stored up. I take off for the woods even though I'm barefoot. They gave me a shirt and pants and no shoes. It takes a while for my eyes to adjust to the darkness, what with me comin' out of the cop station with its bright lights. I don't bother lookin' back. If they're gonna catch me, they're gonna catch me. Stoppin' to look will only slow me down.

This ain't my first time runnin' around in the woods, though I ain't been in the woods over by here before. It don't matter, I got a great sense of direction and can't get lost. I know there's an 86 truck stop about a mile from the police station, so all I gotta do is make my way east through the woods until I see the truck stop and go there. In fact, there's a big ass sign so that truckers can see the place from the highway, so before long I'll see the sign and know exactly where I'm goin'. All I gotta do is walk my happy ass to the truck stop and pretend I'm a lot lizard. I'll find me a trucker and get him to let me in his truck. I'm sure any perverted ol' trucker would let me ride with him if I suck his dick or let him fuck me first. Hell, if he can get these cuffs off, I'll let him fuck my ass if he wants!

From there, I'll just have to wing it, I guess. I ain't got no way to get to Grandaddy's money, so I'll be broke until I figure somethin' out. But I'll make do. Funny thing is, I mighta stayed and let them police take me to prison, the real prison I mean, if that's where I end up, and if I couldn't talk my way out of it. It can't be that bad getting' three meals a day and fuckin' the guard boys from time to time. But I gotta think of the baby growin' inside of me! If they take me to prison and find out I got a baby, they'll prob'ly take my baby from me and I might never see her again! That would be a real shame after all I went through to have her. She needs her Momma, and I need my baby! I'm finally gonna have me a baby, all my own! And I just know it's a girl. I'm gonna name her Jolene too. I can't wait to meet her!

I get to the truck stop and there's two trucks just idlin' there. I walk up to the first truck and knock on the door. Some fat Mexican lookin' guy opens the door. "Can I help you?" he asks, tryin' to play innocent, like he don't know what a lot lizard is.

"Mind if I get a ride? I'm willin' to pay for it if I need to." He lets me in, then I show him the handcuffs. He smiles, his teeth all fucked up, and opens the glove box. Praise Jesus, he's got a handcuff key. I mean, so does Grandaddy, but that doesn't help me now. A lot of people don't realize that all cop handcuffs use the same key. All you have to do is buy a pair of police handcuffs and it comes with the key to get you out of their cuffs too. The nice Mexican man unlocks my cuffs, so I say, "Look I don't have any money to pay for the ride, but I can do anything you want." His shows his fucked up teeth again and pulls out his fat cock. It's real thick, maybe bigger around than it is long, so I worry for my asshole if that's what he wants.

Lucky for me, he's good with regular ol' pussy-pounding. He just pushes his seat back and I straddle him and bounce on his dick a few times. He stares at my tits bouncin', showing off his bad teeth some more. Once he cums in me, I pop off him, letting his cum fall out on his seat as I go back over to the passenger side. I take one of his cigarettes that I saw in his glovebox and light up while he puts his thick brown dick away.

"We leave in the morning," he says and goes to sleep, snorin' all loud. While he's sleeping, I steal his bank card from his wallet. The idiot has the PIN numbers written on it!

The next day, he drives us east and drops me off at another truck stop. Apparently, he was done with his shipment and was on his way back home. There's plenty of trucks here that I could hitch a ride with, but first I need to get a change of clothes, so I go in the truck stop's little shop and find a kid's size t-shirt and some sweats. I pay for it using the trucker's card, then change into my new clothes in the bathroom before shoving my jail clothes in the trash can under some bloody tampons that were already in there. After that, I take out $500 from an ATM at the truck stop, which is the max it lets me do, then ditch the card as well.

So, yeah, I end up changing my mind about hitching another ride and decide to walk to the nearby motel where they take cash. I book a few nights so I can lay low. This is good because I come to find out they're lookin' for me and got my picture on the news and everything! On the TV news, they're talkin' about the house, how it mysteriously exploded the night I was arrested, killing two police officers on the scene (whoops!). On the bright side, they won't know what's going on beyond what they can get out of that bunny bitch who killed Grandaddy and Big Joe.

It's at this motel that I start getting hungry for bunny meat. It's been too long since I've had some, a week it feels like though I know it's only been a few days. This type of hunger makes my teeth itch somethin' awful. The second night I'm here at the motel, I'm just hangin' out at the soda-pop machine waitin' for a bunny when some bunny boy comes over. He invites me to his room where he's got some bourbon, nothin' as good as

Grandaddy's moonshine, but still I haven't had a drink in even longer than I've had the bunny meat so it burns so good. Then he wants to fuck, so I oblige. I get him on the bed and tie his wrists to the headboard with the cop cuffs I kept. I get a bit more creative with his legs, pulling his pants down to his shoes, then tying his pants to the footboard with his belt. He's already hard for me, so I can put the rubber band on his cock right away. I hope his cock tastes as good as it looks!

ACKNOWLEDGEMENTS

Thank you, Momo, for being my biggest fan and first reader, even though the gross stuff is not your cup of tea. Sorry about the Grandaddy blowjob part! I'm glad you pushed through all of this mess. Your notes were extremely helpful as I brought this monstrosity through every iteration and draft into what it is today.

Thanks to NaNoWriMo for helping with my goal and keeping me on task. Until next time!

And, of course, big thanks to anyone who gave this book a chance. Please let me know your thoughts by reviewing on your favorite book review site or sending an email to oscarbradybooks@yahoo.com.

Made in the USA
Monee, IL
27 April 2025